THE
WALKING
FISH

For further information, contact:
Tumblehome Learning, Inc.
P.O. Box 171386
Boston, MA 02117, USA
http://www.tumblehomelearning.com

Library of Congress Control Number: 2014959815

Burk, Rachelle / Burk, Kopel, MD
THE WALKING FISH / Rachelle Burk & Kopel Burk, MD -1st ed

ISBN 978-0-9907829-4-0
1. Children - Fiction 2. Science Fiction 3. Mystery

Cover art/design: Barnas Monteith

Printed in Taiwan

10 9 8 7 6 5 4 3 2 1

THE
WALKING
FISH

Rachelle Burk & Kopel Burk, MD

Tumblehome learning, Inc.

For Barbara Green,
who gave me the courage to write.
And for Kopel—
Renaissance man, role model,
and best uncle in the world.
~ R.B.

For my children,
grandchildren, nieces and nephews,
to whom I have enjoyed
telling my stories for many years.
~ K.B.

CHAPTER 1

When you get right down to it, I only discovered the Walking Fish because Grandpa got sloppy with a chainsaw.

Had he been more careful cutting down the maple tree, he would not have lost most of the fingers of his right hand. "Four of my favorite fingers," he said. Without them, fishing was a bit of a struggle.

"Minnow," he said, "I've been *flounder-ing* with my hooks these days. It would sure be *hand-y* to have you as a fishing partner."

"Ha, ha, Grandpa," I said. "Very punny." He's the king of bad puns. The truth is, he could still cast the line and reel in fish with the best of them, but he now needed help wrestling the squirming worms onto the hooks. Unfortunately, live bait made me squeamish, and he knew it.

It was a sunny, fall day and we drifted, just the two of us, on his little fishing boat on a lake. He leaned forward, elbows on his knobby knees. The faded swordfish tattoo on his forearm wiggled as he drummed his fingers against his other hand. His white hair was thin, but the few wisps poking from his beneath his captain's hat fluttered in the breeze.

Though he was trying to relax, his posture was awkward and unnatural. That's because Grandpa is not a relaxer. He's a fisherman who feels naked without a pole in his hands.

I squeezed my eyes shut against the bright sun as I lay on the wooden bench seat, legs dangling over the side of the boat. My ponytail slurped up the little pool of water from the boat floor like a straw. Unlike Grandpa, I'm an expert relaxer.

The silence that followed gave me the feeling he wasn't just trying to be funny. Maybe he was serious about my being his helper. He was waiting for an answer.

"I don't know, Grandpa. I'm afraid if I start baiting your hooks, that would just open up a whole can of worms." I peeked with one eye to gauge his reaction to my joke. What I saw was a worm dangling over my face.

I shrieked and scrambled upright, batting the squiggly thing away.

"I came prepared in case you said yes," he said, and began to assemble his fishing pole. "You watch," he assured me, "I'll get you *hooked* on fishing yet."

Sure enough, in no time at all, I really was hooked, and Grandpa rewarded me with my very own fishing gear.

****

A few months later, my parents and I drove up the driveway of our summer cabin at Glacial Lake. The shady log-and-stone structure was familiar and inviting. It was built in a clearing about two hundred yards from the lake's edge. Gravel crunched beneath the tires as Dad pulled up to the house. There was no garage, but tall trees along the driveway kept the car from turning into a sauna on hot days.

We unloaded suitcases and boxes from the trunk and hauled them up the steps. The white paint on the front porch had started to peel, but inside the rustic cabin, nothing had changed. An oversized pine table with mismatched chairs stood in a corner of the cozy living room. Sheets covered the overstuffed couch and recliner. I inhaled deeply. The cabin smelled of mothballs, dust, and burnt firewood. I love the scent, yet the first thing my mother always did was to open all the windows to air out the place, and shake out the dusty woven rugs scattered about the wide-planked wood floor.

I went back out to the car to retrieve my fishing pole and tackle box, which I had stashed on the floor of the back seat.

"What did you bring that for?" Dad asked when I deposited the gear near the kitchen door. Mom was busy stocking the refrigerator and cabinets full of gourmet cooking supplies.

"You don't think I'd spend a whole summer at the lake without my fishing stuff, do you?" I said.

Dad shook his head. "Don't you remember? There are no fish in Glacial Lake. If there were, we could certainly convince your grandfather to come with us now and then."

My heart sank. I had planned to supply my family with fresh trout for the grill, and to help Mom invent new fish recipes.

"I'm sure I remember Dr. H saying that the lake was stocked," I said. That's Dr. Holland. He teaches environmental science courses at Glacial Lake University. He and his wife are "lake friends" of my parents. Dad is a junior high school science teacher, so he and Dr. H hit it off from the first time they met.

It was my mother who answered. "No, what he said was that the Department of Fish and Wildlife *tried* to stock it. A number of times, in fact. Every attempt failed. Something about the minerals in the water, right, Fred?" She looked at my father for confirmation. He nodded.

"Maybe some survived," I said hopefully.

Dad shook his head. "Sorry kiddo. Not a chance. This lake is great for swimming, canoeing, and sunbathing. Just don't plan on catching our dinner, unless the guy at the supermarket tosses you a frozen fillet."

I slumped into a kitchen chair. "Well, you never know. I heard they found an alligator in a New York sewer, so maybe I'll find fish in Glacial Lake." I yanked the elastic band from my pony tail. The tangled dark mess that is my hair fell over my face. Hiding behind a curtain of locks allowed me to sulk in semiprivacy.

"Uh oh," said my mother. "Someone is moping."

"I'm *not* moping," I said.

"Hair in the face, dimples have vanished. Those are sure signs."

"Well, can you blame me? I won't be able to fish for months. It'll be the most boring summer in the history of me. If Grandpa comes to visit us at the cabin, I want to go back home with him."

Okay, maybe I *was* moping. Maybe I needed to look at the bright side. After all, it would still be a fun summer as long as I had Darshan to hang out with. We'd go for swims and hikes and bike rides—all the things our families used to do together before his father's accident. I looked across the yard to the Mishras' house next door. "Darshan isn't home," I said. "There's no car in the driveway."

The Mishras are one of the few families who live year-round on the lake, where most of the homes are summer residences or rentals. The rest of the population lives in nearby Glacial Village where the university is located. Like many of the residents, Darshan's family is connected to the local university. Mrs. Mishra teaches Asian literature. Mr. Mishra works in the Information Technology department, making sure all the computer systems throughout the school work properly. He's a good person to know, since my parents are practically computer illiterate. Plus, the Mishras let us log in to their Wi-Fi since we don't have it at the cabin.

Dad settled into the chair opposite mine. "It's Saturday. They're probably out doing stuff. If you have nothing to do till he gets back, this is the perfect opportunity to get a head start on the

4

next school year." He pulled an eighth grade biology book from a box on the floor and slid it to me across the table.

"Very funny, Dad." I tossed it back in the box as if it were a smelly sock.

I gazed out the kitchen window at the dazzling green mountains and rocky cliffs rising above the glistening lake. It reminded me of how I used to make mountains and lakes with my mashed potatoes and gravy. I still would, if my mother ever made plain old mashed 'taters and gravy any more. Instead, she whips up "new red skins with fried garlic and chives" or "double baked stuffed potatoes au gratin." Suddenly I felt hungry, and realized we hadn't stopped for lunch.

"Can I have a snack?"

"Check the cooler on the counter," said Mom. "I made something special."

What now? I thought.

I found something shaped like a toilet paper roll beneath the ice packs and peeled off the aluminum foil. Smoked salmon and goat cheese with dill and capers.

"You know, peanut butter and jelly would have been fine, Mom," I said, biting into the wrap.

My mother writes a column for a popular cooking magazine. In fact, she's somewhat of a celebrity. Her picture appears in every issue, her shoulder length hair youthfully framing her face. She looks a lot like me—small, round-faced, a few freckles across her nose—only her hair is a few shades lighter due to Clairol Hair Color.

Now she has a publishing contract for a gourmet cookbook that she hopes to finish by the end of the summer. She expects it to make her as famous as Martha Stewart or Rachel Ray. Dad and I, plus a few willing friends, are her official tasters.

5

"I'd give it a seven," I said between bites. "More salt, less dill."

The smoked salmon made me think again about fishing.

"I'm going down to the lake," I announced, pushing myself from the table. I grabbed my fishing gear on my way to the back door.

Dad eyed the fishing pole. "In spite of your apparent optimism about catching fish for supper, we'll be having spaghetti tonight."

"Not *spaghetti*, Fred," Mom huffed. "*Linguini Carbonara.*"

"I'm just going to practice my casting," I said. The screen door creaked as I pushed it open.

"Why the net, then?" Dad asked.

"Frogs."

"You are *not* going to create Frog City on the porch again this year," Mom yelled. The screen door banged shut as I raced from the cabin.

CHAPTER 2

I barely recognized our own yard as I darted across the field. The heavy spring rains the month before had dramatically changed the familiar rocky shoreline. Now two ponds, created when the lake overflowed, took up a large area about twenty yards from the edge of Glacial Lake. I figured that in another two or three weeks the pond water would likely evaporate, leaving the grass and stones high and dry and the shoreline back to its usual state.

I kicked off my shoes and waded along the rocky edge of the lake. Clouds had rolled in, making the water appear dark and flat. For a few minutes I cast my fishing line out as far as I could, but I quickly grew tired of it. The new ponds behind me, between the lake and the cabin, looked like they could be fun spots to practice my casting technique. The larger one was about the size of a tennis court, and from one edge I tried a couple of my favorite lures. A white rock peeked up from the water at the far end like a miniature iceberg. I aimed and flicked my pole. Zzzzzzzzz…plop. The lure made a dainty splash within a yard of my target. Darshan would be impressed.

A ripple appeared in the water near a cluster of boulders, only inches from where my hook had landed. I retrieved the net and made my way around the pond to inspect the site. Again, a tiny splash. A raindrop? I examined the hazy sky, now streaked with pink near the horizon. No, those weren't rain clouds.

Standing motionless, I strained to see beneath the surface of the water, my net poised to scoop up the turtle or frog the first moment it made itself visible.

The next movement occurred near the first one, beneath a slab of gray rock. I stepped closer and squinted. The angle of the setting sun made it difficult to see beneath the water.

There it was again. Something definitely crept beneath the boulder. I set down the net, lowered myself onto my belly, and shaded my eyes. The water here was only about a foot and a half deep, and as long as I didn't stir up the mud, I could make out the bottom of the pond.

Swiping my fingertips across the surface to brush away some floating leaves, I was surprised at the coldness of the water. Shouldn't the afternoon sun have warmed this shallow water? Even the lake felt warmer than the pond.

Splish-splash. There it was again. When the water settled once more, my eyes gradually focused on the creature causing the disturbance. It wasn't a frog. It wasn't a turtle.

It was a creature like nothing I had ever seen. A fish! And it appeared to be standing on little legs and waving up at me.

CHAPTER 3

"Oh, oh, oh!" I gasped. The critter seemed to have become aware of me, but instead of swimming away, it began to burrow into the mud under the flat rock. I scrambled to my feet, grabbed the net and scooped wildly beneath the surface, stirring up the silt on the bottom. The net came up empty.

"Stupid, stupid," I scolded myself. The water was now as brown and murky as chocolate milk. I held my breath and scooped blindly this time, aiming for the spot where the fish had been.

Unsuccessful, I stepped into the frigid water, crouched low, and groped around. A cool current flowed against my ankles, which I suspected was caused by the fish's thrashing tail. Again I scraped the net along the bottom. Once, twice, three times I hauled up the net, each time dumping out mud and small stones gathered from the bottom of the pond. On my fourth scoop, something flip-flopped in the mesh.

I caught it! Panting, I waded from the pond, dragging the netting just deep enough beneath the water to keep the fish immersed. My soaked capris clung to my legs and hips.

I glanced around the shore and groaned. No bucket. Oh, well, I'd call Mom or Dad and ask them to bring one down for me. I reached into a pocket and drew out my cell phone.

The screen was blank. My soggy pants had shorted the circuit.

Oops. Another ruined phone. My parents were going to kill me. I sighed and slipped it back into my pocket.

Gathering stones with my free hand, I piled them onto the handle of the net to anchor it on the shore, while the fish remained safely beneath the water in the netting. The metal rim of the net hovered just above the surface of the pond so that the fish couldn't swim out.

When I was satisfied that my catch was secure, I crouched down to study it. Something wasn't right. Not at all. I bent in for a closer look, so close that I nearly snorted water up my nostrils. What on earth had I caught? My heart began to pound. Never before had I seen a fish like this. A moment later, I took off running, still barefoot, toward the cabin.

CHAPTER 4

I burst through the screen door into the kitchen. "Mom, Dad, come quick, I caught a fish!"

My father had been changing a light bulb in the pantry, and stepped down from the stool. "A shark? A whale?" he asked, tossing the dead bulb into the trash beneath the sink.

"A whale isn't a fish. And I'm serious. Please, Dad, come see," I pleaded. I hopped across the kitchen and glanced around the living room. "Where's Mom?"

"We forgot to bring toilet paper, so she went to the store. Show me what you found." He slipped his bare feet into the yellow flowered flip-flops that my mother keeps near the back door.

The small trash can beneath the kitchen sink was the closest thing we had to a bucket, so I removed the garbage-filled plastic liner from it. Hugging the empty can to my chest, I sprinted like a cheetah through the yard toward the pond. My father, on the other hand, strolled leisurely behind me like a camel through a hot desert. I hollered over my shoulder. "Hurry, Dad. You're so slow!" The sun was setting now, smearing the sky with orange and pink hues. I wanted to get there before it got dark. Even though my father sped up, my toddler cousin could have beaten him in a race. My mother's flip-flops sure weren't helping his speed.

When I reached the far side of the pond I frantically threw off the stones that anchored the handle in place, and raised the net. It was empty.

"AHHHH! It's escaped!" I flung the net and pulled at my hair. My father, hands clasped behind his back, watched me with amusement as I paced in frustration. "Dad, I did catch a fish, I swear it. How could it get away?"

"Sorry, honey," he said with a shrug, "I guess it jumped out. What was it anyway? A trout? A bluegill? I think those are the kinds they tried to stock the lake with. I guess some survived after all. That means I may have been wr...wr...wr...." He pretended that he couldn't spit out the word "wrong," but I was in no mood for his joking. My lips trembled, and when I didn't reply, he sat cross-legged on the weedy ground next to my useless pile of rocks. He reached up to me. I collapsed beside him and buried my face in his shoulder.

"It didn't look anything like either of those fish. I know this sounds crazy, but it looked like it didn't have eyes. At least not that I could see. Seriously, everything about it was..." I straightened up and looked into Dad's eyes. "It was all wrong, like something Picasso would paint."

"It was probably a bullfrog or something." He stroked my hair, like someone trying to calm a crying baby.

"Dad, I know a frog from a fish," I snapped, pushing his hand away. I rose and kicked a stone with my bare foot. "And it was a funny looking fish, that's for sure."

CHAPTER 5

"*Why* are you so sure fish can't live in Glacial Lake?" I whined. "And don't tell me to look it up."

My father's broad shoulders stiffened. It drives him crazy when I whine. Of course, when I'm feeling whiny, driving him crazy is quite satisfying. We were having a late dinner on the screened back porch. It's where we have nearly all our meals, even when it rains. Dad continued to insist that what I found couldn't have been a fish. Or if it was, someone had to have put it in the pond.

"The mineral content is too high."

"Hmph. I know for a fact that fish can live in water like that," I said, pushing Mom's experimental pretzel-crusted chicken around on my plate. "Take, for instance, the Devil's Hole Pupfish, a teensy-weensy, inch-long fish found only in a cavern in the desert of Death Valley. *So there!*"

My father bobbed his head thoughtfully. He was impressed. "And where did you learn that little tidbit of trivia?"

"*Fishing Today Magazine*. Grandpa has a subscription. There's a feature column about cool, strange fish around the world."

"That's great. Next time you're in Death Valley, catch us a few dozen pupfish and we'll fry them up as a snack. However, this doesn't change the fact that no fish live in Glacial Lake."

"But *why*?"

"Dr. Holland explained it couple years ago."

"I was just a kid then. Tell me again."

He wiggled, getting comfortable in his chair. He's always happy when the conversation turns to science. Dad teaches science and math at my middle school. My friends say I'm lucky to have his expert help with my homework. I believe it's the worst possible luck to have to go to school where my own father teaches.

On the other hand, I love when he tries out new projects on me. Once we used a raw potato to create electricity, which ran a clock for over a week. We made magnets out of nails and a battery and volcanic eruptions from mixing baking soda and vinegar. I discovered which things, when combined, would fizz, bubble, pop, spark, explode or change colors. All in all, it isn't so bad being an only child with a playmate like my dad. That is, when he isn't annoying, bossing, embarrassing, or teasing me.

He cleared his throat. "Billions of years ago, this whole area was covered by water." He swept his hand across the mountain landscape. I could envision him in front of his science class, waving his arms and gesturing at maps and charts. Dad could make neutrons sound thrilling, and his excitement was contagious.

"Everything you see here was under water, teeming with all sorts of marine life. As sea creatures died, their shells and bones were deposited in the shallow seas along continental shelves. This material became the limestone we find in all of the surrounding mountains." He paused, glancing at me. "Still with me?"

"Yep, I'm listening. I'll let you know if I fall asleep."

My father chuckled. "All right, you do that. Now, where was I?"

"Dead fish, limestone, blah, blah, blah."

"Right." He pushed away from the table and began to pace. "At some point, the ocean floor was lifted up as areas deep underground began to move."

"What made them move?" I asked.

"You remember learning about tectonic plates, right?"

14

"Sure. When they moved, sometimes even whole continents shifted," I said.

"Excellent." The corner of his mouth turned up. Correct answers make him happy. "Each time one plate slipped under another, earthquakes raised the land a bit higher, forming these mountains in a process that spanned millions of years. Other wild things happened as well, like volcanoes spewing up molten rock. Pshoo! Pshoo!" Dad's arms flailed around to simulate a lava eruption. "Then, the lava hardened as it cooled, creating—"

"Ignorant rock!" I proudly finished the sentence.

"Huh?" He tilted his head with a puzzled look.

"You know," I said, "when lava from volcanoes hardens, it makes ignorant rock."

He burst out laughing. "Oh, you mean 'igneous' rock?"

I grew silent. *That* is what I mean by his teasing.

Mom looked up from her plate to find my expression as hard as, well, ignorant rock. She slapped my father's arm. "Stop laughing at her, Fred. You know she hates that."

"Sorry," he said. Though judging by his grin, I doubted that he was. "Do you want me to go on?"

"Whatever."

"Okay. Over time the earth's temperature dropped. There were ice ages when so much snow accumulated that it became packed and hardened into massive mountains of ice."

"Glaciers," I said, hoping to redeem myself.

"Good girl," said Dad. "You must have been awake for that lesson."

"Most of it. Then what?"

"Massive glaciers began to move down from the mountains toward the sea, scouring and scraping the landscape and exposing the volcanic rock beneath. If you take a look at the surrounding mountains now, you can see those exposed areas."

My mother chimed in. "When you were small, you used to see animal shapes and faces in those bald, rocky spots on the mountains."

There was still just enough daylight left to see them from where we sat.

"Yeah, I remember. I even talked to them. They were my imaginary friends."

"Really?" Mom put a hand over her heart and wrinkled her nose. "That's so cute."

I batted my eyes. "I know. I'm totally adorable. Now let Dad finish."

My father scratched his head. "Where was I?"

"Lakes, volcanic rock, blah, blah, blah."

"Right. Then the earth's temperature warmed and the ice melted, once again forming lakes and rivers. When rainwater and streams flowed over the igneous rock, it washed high concentrations of minerals such as iron, copper, sulfur, etcetera, into the lake. This is what created the hostile environment for fish."

"What do you mean, 'hostile environment'?" I asked. By now Dad's dinner was getting cold. I had already cleaned my plate and was beginning to pick at his. He was too busy lecturing to notice.

"In this case, it means that the level of minerals in the water is too high for fish to survive."

"Can't the fish get used to it? My science teacher says animals adapt over time."

"That takes millions of years."

"It *has* been millions of years," I said. "You just said so."

"Well, this time they didn't manage to make the change, I guess."

I was quiet for a few moments. "Remember those fossils and seashells that we found way up in the mountains a few years ago? I never could figure out how they got up there."

"Now you know," he said with finality. "Want to go fossil hunting again this summer?"

"Okay, but I'd rather go fishing." I sighed, and carried the plates into the kitchen to wash the dishes.

****

"Mom and Dad don't believe me, Grandpa, but it's true. I really did catch a freaky fish."

I had shut myself in my room with Mom's cell phone—since mine was kaput—and told him every detail of the day. Unloading my woes on Grandpa usually made me feel better. My head dangled off the side of the bed, and my hair spilled over the bare pine floor. A red t-shirt, draped over my bedside lamp, cast a peaceful warm glow over the room.

"Of course you did, dear. We all have a story about the one that got away. Did I ever tell you the time I caught a mermaid? I used a diamond ring as bait, but the darned thing stole the jewel and slipped from my net."

"Oh, brother," I sighed. I flipped myself upright. "Goodnight, Grandpa."

"Goodnight, Minnow."

****

17

That night I dreamed I was fishing on a sailboat and caught a talking trout. The fish was psychic and, when I jiggled it like a Magic 8-Ball, it gave me answers to any problem. The scene switched, and I was on the beach speaking to a group of world leaders about the nutritional value of the magic fish. Suddenly, an angry old man grabbed the microphone and began scolding me for not wearing sunscreen. I woke in a pool of drool.

"Uh oh," Mom said when I plodded into the kitchen. "Today's mood report: Gray with a chance of teardrops." She pushed the hair from my face and tucked it behind my ears. "Still disappointed about the fish, I see."

I shrugged and kept my gaze at the floor. Grandpa's pep talk hadn't stuck.

Mom clapped her hands loudly, as if she had an exciting announcement. "How about I fix you some French crepes?" In a tempting tone she sang, "Paper thin, with fresh blueberry compote."

She must be starting the breakfast chapter of her cookbook, I thought. This meant we'd probably be eating breakfast three meals a day as she tried out new recipes.

I shook my head. "Not for me, thanks. I saw a car next door in the driveway, so I'm heading over to see Darshan. He'll help me catch the fish again, and you'll see I wasn't making it up."

"Don't be disappointed if you don't find anything," Mom said.

Grandpa wouldn't have said that. He'd have cheered me on. Undeterred, I downed a glass of orange juice and headed to the door.

Mom called out, "Tell his parents they should all come for dinner this weekend. I'm trying out a new vegetarian recipe and need someone to test it on."

Racing across the field that connected our properties, I leapt over dandelions and wild violets, trying not to crush them under my feet. When I reached Darshan's back porch, I bounded up the wheelchair ramp beside the wooden steps. Hydrangea vines climbed up each side of the stairs and were beginning to creep across the porch floor. A colored glass wind chime made dainty tinkling music in the gentle breeze.

I knocked on the door.

"Alexis, hello! Welcome back!" said Mrs. Mishra. She pulled me to her in a tight hug. Her clothes and hair were saturated with the wonderful aroma of exotic spices.

Mr. Mishra rolled up behind her in his motorized wheelchair. "Is that Alexis I hear? It is you! When did you get to town?"

Before I could answer, Darshan squeezed past his parents and tugged my sleeve. "It's about time you got in town. It's been so boring around here that I was losing my mind."

Now we were all crowded in the doorway. Mrs. Mishra rolled her eyes. "Don't be so dramatic, Darshan. You've only been out of school for three days."

"That's true, dear," said her husband, "but you must remember those are 'kid days,' which are equivalent to about a month of adult days."

Darshan covered his eyes and shook his head. "Can I go now, Amma?" he asked.

"Don't be rude, Darshan. Invite her in for tea."

I inhaled deeply. The sweet smell of cardamom and ginger wafted from the kitchen. I licked my lips, and for a moment I forgot about the fish.

Mrs. Mishra took my hand. "Come, Alexis, sit. Tell us what you have been up to."

"Okay, thanks, Mrs. Mishra." I brushed past Darshan and followed his mother into the kitchen. Their house is much bigger and more modern than our cabin, with two levels and four big bedrooms. The stairway had an electric chair lift, though Mr. Mishra rarely used it since they converted the back den into a big master bedroom suite.

Darshan's mom put a cup of masala tea in front of me at the kitchen table and slipped from the room, giving Darshan and me some privacy. I loved the hot, tongue-tickling drink—milky and sweet with a spicy bite. Darshan drew in a spiral sketchpad and chatted about the past school year. He had gotten a job walking a neighbor's dog after school, made the soccer team, and was involved in starting an art club. Compared to him, I looked like a lazy bum.

"You're never without that drawing pad, are you?" I said. "What are you working on now?"

Wordlessly, he slid the picture toward me. It was an impressively detailed sketch of an older woman with a pair of reading glasses, attached to a jeweled chain, perched on the bridge of her nose. What struck me the most was the expression on the woman's face—the raised eyebrows and slightly parted lips. I rubbed my chin, studying the picture. "She looks so...so..."

Darshan leaned forward. "Embarrassed?"

"Hmm...no, more like startled."

He slumped back in his chair. "Ugh. I was going for 'embarrassed.' I've been working on facial expressions, and this one is the hardest." With frustration, he took the pad back from me, and rubbed his eraser across the subject's eyes.

I reached into a bowl of spicy nuts and seeds—everything in this house was deliciously spicy—and tossed a few into my mouth. I continued to watch Darshan with fascination as he worked on

20

his picture. "Who is that anyway? And what's she embarrassed about?"

"It's a picture of my English teacher after she farted."

"Darshan!" scolded his mother, who had been eavesdropping from the living room. I laughed, which launched a nut from my mouth across the glass table. It landed in Darshan's lap. He tossed it back and it bounced off my forehead.

"Well it's true," he said with a smirk. "The room was real quiet because we were taking a test, so everyone heard it. The look on her face will be forever burned in my brain. My job now is to get it on paper." We both doubled over in a fit of giggles.

I gathered our empty tea cups and carried them to the sink. Mrs. Mishra rushed in. "Leave it. I'll take care of it," she said, taking the cups from me and waving us off. "Okay you two, out. It's too pretty a day to stay inside."

"Okay, but can we borrow a cooler?" I asked. "Something with a lid. I'm going to catch a fish."

Mrs. Mishra tilted her head and squinted at me inquisitively. "Alex, you know there aren't any—"

"Oh, yes, there *are!*" I interrupted. My hands flew to my mouth. "Oh, sorry, Mrs. Mishra...I mean, you're right that fish haven't lived in the lake before, but I definitely saw one yesterday. Not in the lake itself, actually. It was in the big pond that's appeared in front of the lake, so I guess it probably got trapped, you know, when the lake overflowed and all. Honestly, it was some kind of strange, alien fish, but it got away, so I have to catch it again." I drew in a deep breath, my eyes pivoting between Darshan and his mom.

For a long moment, they stared at me like I was totally nuts. Finally, Mrs. Mishra shrugged and said, "The cooler is in the garage."

I followed Darshan through a breezeway off the kitchen into the garage that they used for storage and as a workshop.

Mr. Mishra was inside tinkering with a computer. The machine's guts were spread out onto a workbench beneath a bright fluorescent light. He hovered over it with his skinny tools, like a doctor performing delicate surgery.

"I caught a fish yesterday, Mr. Mishra," I announced.

He inspected some electronic part that he held up with narrow tweezers. "Did you, now? Well good for you," he said without looking up.

I whispered to Darshan. "Your parents don't believe me, either."

"I wouldn't worry about it," he said as he sifted through a pile of stuff. "When we catch it again they'll all have to eat their words."

I was so grateful for his confidence that I wanted to throw my arms around him. Instead I said, "By the way, Dar, your drawings are good. *Really* good. You've gotten a lot better since last year."

"Thanks. I've been practicing. I want to be an illustrator when I grow up." He climbed over a leaf blower, moved a boogie board, and pulled out a large red cooler with a white lid.

"Last summer you said you wanted to be a veterinarian."

"That was before I saw my friend's cat cough up a hairball." He wrinkled his nose. "It was really gross. Now I'm going to be an illustrator."

We said goodbye to his dad and hurried toward to the pond, each holding a handle of the huge cooler. "Why do we need something so big?" Darshan asked. "My mother has a pail in the laundry room."

"Obviously the fish jumped out of the net. I don't want to chance it jumping from a shallow pail," I said. "This has a lid, plus more room for it to swim around."

We passed Mrs. Mishra's vegetable garden, with its sweet fragrance of cilantro and parsley. Leafy tomato plants clung to cages, and wide-leaf vines crept along the ground. By late summer Mrs. Mishra would bring over baskets of squash, tomatoes, and string beans.

Three summers ago their family had installed a fish pond in this very spot. A few months before, a car accident on an icy mountain road had left Mr. Mishra's legs permanently paralyzed, and his wife decided that he needed a serene spot to relax as he recovered. We all knew it was she who needed the serenity the most. Mrs. Mishra had never totally recovered from her husband's trauma, and worried obsessively about him and her son.

One day, a few weeks after the pond was completed, Darshan's parents sat beside it sipping tea, hypnotized by the spotted koi that glided through the glistening water. In one split second, the spell was broken when a blue heron swooped down and snatched one of the exotic fish. We could hear Mrs. Mishra's horrible shriek all the way from our house. Then, a night or two later, their family watched helplessly as a raccoon carried off another wiggling fish. Within a week, wild animals had made meals of every last fish in the pond.

Horrified and heartbroken, Mrs. Mishra couldn't sleep. The car accident had already made her anxious about her husband and overprotective of her son. New worries about kidnapped fish were more than she wanted to bear, so she ordered a landscaping company to fill in the pond with topsoil. Now a vegetable garden grows where the pond had been.

"Now my mom complains about rabbits and deer nibbling on her lettuce," Darshan said, "but at least they don't freak her out the way those 'murderous creatures' did."

We set the cooler on the bank of the big pond. It was a little past nine and the sun had risen above the mountains. The morning light played on the surface of the lake, but both ponds remained in the shadows. Soon the sun would be high enough to bathe the whole area with warm, bright sunshine. At this hour, though, it was still nippy, and I was sorry I had not worn a sweatshirt.

Darshan retrieved the net that I had left there the day before. We circled the pond, scanned the water, and tossed in pebbles to see if some creature might reveal itself.

"Who am I fooling?" I said after a few fruitless minutes. "We'll never find it." I skimmed a rock across the surface of the pond.

"If you caught it once, we can catch it again," said Darshan. With focused determination, he edged his way around the pond, his eyes fixed on the water.

"At least *you* believe me," I said. "My father seems convinced that I caught a water rat."

Eventually we took off our shoes and stepped into the chilly water. "Careful," Darshan warned, "Don't stir up the muck on the bottom." He sure didn't have to remind me. Slowly we waded to the center, floating the cooler along with us like a little boat.

"Over there!" I pointed. "Something darted just beneath the surface."

It was the fish, I just knew it.

"Where? I don't see it," he said, following my finger.

"There…I think." We stood motionless. Darshan readied the net.

Water bugs skated here and there atop the water. After a while, we concluded that what I had seen must have been one of those bugs. Just in case, I poked around in the mud with my toes. "Nothing."

Darshan gestured toward the opposite side. "You say you caught the fish near a boulder. Is that the one? Maybe we should start over there."

We dipped the cooler to fill it halfway, and set it on the shore by the boulder before beginning a more systematic search. "Here, fishy, fishy…come out fishy, fishy," I chanted, stopping every foot or so to scan beneath the surface. The area where I had first spotted the creature was still in the shade, so I bent low and squinted into the darkness while my eyes adjusted. Near the boulder, my right foot sunk into squishy mud and rested at the edge of a thin, flat rock. I worked my toes beneath it until I was able to lift the edge.

At first I was startled by a shocking rush of icy water. Then something brushed against my foot. I jerked back, nearly losing my balance. Darshan caught my arm to steady me. Silt clouded the water as the rock fell back into place.

"What? What is it?" he asked.

"I felt…something," I whispered. I hovered over the pond, as motionless as the towering mountains. For several long minutes we remained frozen, our eyes never leaving the water. When the mud finally settled, we saw it.

CHAPTER 6

The fish's fins fluttered ever so slightly, keeping it hovering in one spot. Long, catfish-like feelers waved about, tickling my ankle. I held my breath. Suddenly, the creature crawled over my foot. I slapped both hands over my mouth to stifle a scream when, without a word, Darshan swooped down and netted the fish.

"We got it!" I shouted.

Darshan flipped the net into the cooler. While he stood calm and composed, I hollered and danced until my parents raced from the porch to see what the commotion was about.

Though my dad moves like a sloth, my mom can sprint like a gazelle, so she arrived first. I pointed into the cooler. "Check it out!"

The fish swam frantically along the bottom, investigating its prison with two long whiskers. Reaching one end, it tried to scamper up the side with four wide fins shaped curiously like little duck feet. The four of us hovered over the cooler, studying the catch.

"Oh, my word!" said Mom. "It has no eyes."

We all leaned in to examine the creature more closely. It was odd in so many ways.

"What's that hole behind its head?" Darshan asked. "It looks kind of like a whale or dolphin's blowhole."

Dad removed his glasses and practically stuck his nose in the water. "Blowhole? That's bizarre." He crinkled his brow and shook his head. "No…fish don't have blowholes. But…" He paused and rubbed his chin. "…but if it *is* a blowhole, that could mean this fish has some sort of lung. Hard to fathom." His voice trailed off, like he was in a faraway place.

I dropped to my knees beside the cooler, hands grasping the sides. "It's like an alien from another world," I gushed.

"A mysterious creature, indeed," said my father. "You've got quite a prize in there. We'd better get it to a safe place and call Dr. Holland."

I straightened up and poked my father's chest. "I *told* you it was a weird fish."

"That's for sure," agreed Mom. "Duck feet, dolphin blow-hole, and blind as a bat. It couldn't get any weirder. When you first described it to your father, I was sure it was all in your head. First imaginary friends on the sides of the mountains, now an imaginary fish."

"Let's put it in the bathtub," I suggested.

"Great idea," said Dad. "We need to fill it with water from the pond, not the faucet."

While I waited with the fish, Darshan fetched a bucket from his laundry room as well as an empty, well-rinsed, five-gallon laundry detergent container. My mother brought down a huge soup pot and a juice pitcher, while my father salvaged two big milk jugs from a neighbor's recycle bin.

"Duh, why not use our own recycle bin, or a garbage can?" I suggested.

Mom and Dad looked at each other. "I'll get the garbage can from the driveway," said my father. "It has wheels."

It took the better part of an hour to carry up enough water to fill the tub. Mom and I each held a handle of the cooler that held the fish. With the lid on, we carried it to the house and left it beside the tub. Then we returned to the pond to fill the bucket and milk jugs with water. Dad and Darshan tried to haul the garbage can filled with water, but it was too heavy. They emptied it little by little till it was about a third full, light enough to roll. They inched it all the way to the house and lugged it up the steps. By the time they got it to the bathroom, Mom and I had already made three trips with our bucket and jugs.

The old bathtub stood on four claw-shaped feet. It was so high that, until the previous year, I needed a step stool to climb into it. Even now, still very short for my age, I practically needed gymnastic skills to swing my legs over the side of the tub to get into it.

Once the tub was filled, my father removed the lid of the cooler. He tipped it over the tub, letting the water flow gently down. The fish sank like a stone and lay motionless at the bottom.

"We killed it!" I gasped. Since it had no eyes to indicate signs of life, only its gills, whiskers and fins gave us any clue, and those appeared still and lifeless. We stood around the tub, collectively holding our breath.

A moment later, the hole behind the fish's head flared, its whiskers wiggled, and soon it was gliding across the porcelain.

"I guess my bubble bath will have to wait," I said, sighing with relief.

My father pulled out his phone. "We need to call Dr. Holland."

CHAPTER 7

My dad put the phone on speaker so everyone could hear. Mom sat on the toilet lid, Darshan leaned against the door frame, and I perched on the edge of the tub.

"Hey, David, this is Fred Byron. How are you and Sylvia?"

"Fred, good to hear from you," said Dr. Holland. "We're fine. Sylvia is out in her garden as usual. Did you know it was just featured in *Home and Garden Magazine?*"

"No surprise," said Dad. "Her garden is already famous in Glacial Village. Now it'll be famous in the whole country."

Why couldn't he get to the point? I motioned impatiently at the tub. He waved me off with a look of annoyance, and let Dr. Holland continue the idle chitchat.

"Yes, we've seen quite an increase in traffic down our street," said Dr. Holland. "The address wasn't in the magazine, but the town residents seem to be pointing tourists our way. So, are you folks in town yet?"

"Sure are. Got in yesterday. We're looking forward to having you over."

Now I thrust my hands to my hips and mouthed, "Tell him, *please!*"

My father held up a "wait-a-minute" finger. After another few moments of small talk he said, "Listen, David, there's something in particular I'm calling about. What would you say if I told you that Alex caught a fish near the lake about an hour ago?"

"I would say that you're trying to pull my leg," said Dr. Holland.

29

"Well, I'm serious," said Dad.

"You know the history of that lake," Dr. Holland said. "There are no natural fish in it, and there have been a number of attempts to stock it with all sorts of fish. None have lived more than a few days."

My father leaned back against the sink. "Are you sure about that?" He winked at me, and I could barely hold back my giggles.

"Absolutely," said Dr. Holland. "Maybe someone, a visitor perhaps, put fish in recently. If so, they're highly unlikely to survive more than a few days. The levels of minerals and elements washed down from the mountains are too concentrated for fish to survive. It's uninhabitable."

"So you're saying nothing can live in it?" asked Dad.

"I didn't say *nothing*, Fred. There's a type of tiny shrimp, some bacteria and other small organisms. But Glacial Lake water is toxic to all fish otherwise native to this area. So whatever fool put that fish in there never bothered to check the lake's history. If someone's trying to stock the lake again, I can guarantee that this experiment will be no more successful than the other half a dozen or so attempts. What kind of fish is it anyway?"

"Why don't I let Alex tell you about it?" Dad held the phone out to me. I sprang from my perch on the tub and grabbed it.

"Hi, Dr. H. I caught a fish, all right! It's pinkish-white, about ten inches long, has three fins on top, and two long whiskers." I purposely left out the coolest stuff, to build up suspense.

"Some sort of catfish, maybe?" he asked.

"I don't think so."

Darshan tugged my elbow. "Alex, tell him about the eyes,"

I put my hand over the speaker. "I'm getting there," I whispered. "Oh, yeah, Dr. H, did I mention it has no eyes?"

"No eyes?"

Darshan nudged my shoulder. "And the feet! Tell him."

I swatted his hand away. "And another thing. It has feet, or something like it. And ask me about the freaky little hole behind its head. Totally crazy, right, Dr. H?"

There was a long pause on the other end of the line. I could hear Dr. Holland's deep breathing as the information sank in.

"If it's okay with all of you, I'd like to come right over."

CHAPTER 8

Darshan took my place on the side of the bathtub to sketch a picture of the fish from above. The rest of us gathered around to watch the strange creature explore the old porcelain tub with its long whiskers.

"See?" I said to Dr. Holland. "When it's not swimming it uses its little foot-fins to crawl around the tub."

Even this early in the summer Dr. Holland's leathery skin was deeply tanned. He ran a hand through the silver hair that spilled over the back of his collar. All he kept saying was, "Hm-mmm…." As he pondered the animal, he slipped a pipe from his breast pocket and held it in the corner of his mouth. He didn't light it. In fact, he didn't even put in any tobacco.

"It appears to be some kind of prehistoric fish," Dr. Holland said finally. "It's not like anything I've seen before. Not a live specimen, anyway. I certainly don't imagine that anyone would have dumped it in the lake on purpose." He hovered closer for a better view and cocked his head. "I don't want to jump to any conclusions, but a fish fossil with similar characteristics was found in this area about forty years ago. It's the only one ever found, and it's on display at the campus museum. We call it the 'Walking Fish' because of its foot-like appendages, a lot like the ones on your fish here." He paused and looked at each of us as if to make sure we followed. "This fish could be a survivor of this species, which was presumed to be extinct, or perhaps a relative that evolved from it. It'll take some research to determine that." Dr. Holland slipped the pipe back into his pocket and faced me. "Tell me again what part of the lake you caught it in."

"Actually, it wasn't in the lake," I said. "Darshan and I caught it in a pond next to the lake."

"Show me." He stepped aside so I could lead the way from the bathroom.

The five of us walked outside. "See," I said, pointing to the two ponds. "They weren't here before. The lake overflowed from all the spring rain."

"She's right," added Darshan. "At first, when the water receded, it left one big pond. That was before the Byrons got here. As it dried more, the big pond became two separate smaller ones. The littler one seems to be shrinking a lot faster."

Dr. Holland stood at the edge of the big pond, his eyes bouncing between the lake, the pond, and the mountains. *Why does he keep looking at the mountains?* I wondered. He drew out his pipe again and tapped the stem against his teeth.

"I have a hunch…" he said at last.

We waited patiently for him to go on. Now his gaze rested only on the mountains. Finally he pointed his pipe at the tallest peak.

"I have a hunch that one of those mountains might have an underground lake or pond filled with a school of these fish. Somehow, the record-high rainfall caused your fish to be washed down to Glacial Lake. We know there are rivers and ponds in some of the caves, though in the twenty years I've lived and worked on this lake I have never heard of fish in any of them. A few shrimp, maybe, but not fish."

For the next hour, we strolled around the ponds and the bank of the lake, theorizing about how the fish might have gotten trapped.

"We'll have to deploy a team to check the lake again, of course," said Dr. Holland. "If one fish was somehow washed down from up there, I suspect there could be others." He paced at the edge of the pond and chattered rapidly, more to himself than to anyone else. "This is big, very big. We need to get this fish to the university," he said, pulling his phone from his pocket. Then he stopped and widened his eyes at me, as if realizing for the first time that I was there. "Oh, sorry. Is that okay with you, Alex? It is, after all, *your* fish. But hopefully, at the university, we can keep it safe and healthy as we study it."

I shrugged. "Well, it's not like I can keep it in our bathtub forever. Just promise I can visit it."

Dr. Holland tried to call his boss, and left a voice message when he received no answer. Then he made a couple more calls to arrange for a truck to transport the fish to the campus aquarium.

We gathered again in the bathroom to wait. I sat on the toilet lid, and Darshan returned to sketching the fish from his spot on the side of the tub. Mom peered over his shoulder at the drawing.

"Darshan, that's amazing. May I?" she asked. He held out the pad and she took it from him to examine it more closely. Mom turned the picture around for the rest of us to admire. "Look what he drew!" With only a pencil, he had captured the fine details of the fish from a top view: its glossy skin, the translucent and vein-lined fins, its delicate feelers, and the small, puckered dimple atop its head.

"You have quite a talent," said Dr. Holland.

Darshan lowered his head, smiling shyly. "Thanks," he murmured.

I piped up. "He's going to be a cartoonist, you know."

"No, not a cartoonist," he quickly corrected. "An illustrator."

"Oh?" My dad raised his eyebrows. "I thought you wanted to be a veterinarian."

"I've changed my mind," said Darshan.

"Yeah," I added. "Did you know that cats vomit hairballs? Yuck."

Embarrassed by the attention, Darshan changed the subject. "What's going to happen to the fish once it's at the university?"

We looked to Dr. Holland for the answer. He was leaning against the door frame, absentmindedly gnawing on the stem of his pipe. "I think it's important that the fish's new home be as close to its natural conditions as possible," he explained. "Of course, we can't be sure what that is. It seems to be doing fine in the pond water, so the best we can do for now is to try to mimic that environment. We want to make life as smooth and easy for the Alex Fish as we can."

My mouth dropped open. "Alex Fish?"

He squeezed my shoulder. "Oh, I'm sure we'll attach a scientific name to it eventually—assuming of course it's not an already identified species that I simply haven't heard about. As I said, it could also be a live specimen of the Walking Fish fossil I mentioned before. For now, I'll just call it the Alex Fish after its discoverer." He winked at me. "Get ready! This will undoubtedly make the news—television, newspapers, you'll see."

"Whoa, I'll be famous!" I said.

Mom feigned exasperation. "Newspapers? TV? I came up to Glacial Lake for peace and quiet!" Her eyes gleamed, and in spite of her protests, I could tell she was as excited as the rest of us.

"Dr. H, are you going to hunt for more fish?" I asked.

"Oh, yes, probably for days and weeks to come."

From the bathroom window I saw a van, like a small moving truck, pull into the driveway. Two students from the university, a male and a female, got out. "They're here," I said.

35

Soon the team assembled around the tub. Now there were seven people crowded in the small bathroom. The group oohed and aahed over the amazing fish.

When they explained how they would get it to the campus, Darshan asked, "Why can't you just take it in the cooler?"

"It could be stressful for the fish to be trapped for the ride in something so small," Dr. Holland answered. "Or worse, it could get injured sloshing back and forth during the drive. The department has a special marine transport truck, so there's no need to take any chances."

For the second time that day, we found ourselves hauling water from the pond. In an hour, we had filled the aquarium and three barrels in the back of the truck.

The girl wiped her forehead with her shirt sleeve and said, "I think we're ready for the fish."

Back to the bathroom.

"Can I have a minute alone with it?" I asked.

They all eyed me questioningly.

"You're kidding, right?" my father asked.

"No, I want to have a heart-to-heart talk with it about its future."

Now everyone was sure to think I was nuts. I blushed and said, "Okay, if you must know, I have to use the toilet. There's only one bathroom in this house and it's been pretty crowded for the past few hours. Do you *mind?*" I flicked a hand to shoo everyone out.

"That's fine," said Dr. Holland. "I should try to call Dr. Mertz again, anyway."

Watching my fish from the porcelain throne, it was hard to believe I might have actually discovered a new, live species of fish. That would absolutely get me extra credit in science class.

36

"The *Alex Fish*. The *Alexis Byron Fish*," I whispered. Either way, I liked the sound of it. "I have got to call Grandpa and tell him about you," I said, watching it like a proud mother as it glided 'round and 'round the tub, wiggling its adorable whiskers.

From out in the hallway Dad bellowed, "What's taking her so long? Is she reading a book?"

I opened the door. "As a matter of fact, I was. *One Fish, Two Fish* was its favorite. I promised to read it *Moby Dick* next."

When the team reassembled around the tub, one of the students—a guy with uncombed blond hair, a patchy beard, and painted skin—offered me a net. The octopus tattoo on his arm had tentacles that extended down all of his fingers. It gave the appearance that the octopus was holding the net. "Do you want to do the honors?" he asked.

I fumbled with the handle. My hands trembled. "Let Darshan do it. He's the one who scooped it from the pond, so he has more experience." I thrust the net into his hands.

Darshan slipped the net beneath the fish and flipped it gently into the same cooler we had used to cart it to the house.

Octopus Guy carried it out and climbed into the back of the truck. From the outside, it looked no different from a typical moving van. But on the inside, it had a large, Plexiglas aquarium built into the wall.

There were a couple of possible routes to the campus. We could drive slowly on the back roads without worrying about holding up traffic. But that option would be long and bumpy. In the end, Dr. Holland decided we should take the two-lane highway since the smoother ride would be less likely to stress the fish. If the snail's pace bothered other drivers, too bad.

Dr. Holland headed toward his car. "You folks coming along?"

I faced my father, palms pressed together pleadingly. "Can we, Dad, please?"

He considered. "There's pond water splashed all through the house. Somebody has to clean the tub and mop up the wood floors before this place starts to smell like a fishing pier."

I put on my best sad-puppy face.

"You and Darshan go," Mom said. "Your father and I can clean up."

CHAPTER 9

The truck crept along the main highway at a speed of twenty miles per hour. Dr. Holland, Darshan and I followed behind in Dr. Holland's Prius. When the truck began the climb up a steep part of the mountain road, our speed dropped to a crawl. Drivers behind us honked with irritation. I wondered if we'd possibly get there before dark.

"I'm hungry," I announced.

"You're always hungry," said Darshan. "As much as you eat, it's a mystery how you can be as thin as a toothpick."

I straightened my shoulders. "The word is *petite*," I said. "Besides, we forgot to eat lunch and it's nearly time for dinner."

As if on cue, Darshan's stomach rumbled. "Good point. Hey, Dr. Holland, do you think you can pass the fish truck?"

When we reached a spot where Dr. Holland could see well into the oncoming traffic lane, he pulled around the truck. We made it to the university far ahead of the fish, with enough time to spare to get a snack at the campus café.

"Dr. H, do you really think there's an underground lake in one of those mountains?" I asked between bites of nacho chips. "And maybe schools of those fish that no one ever saw before?"

"That's my hypothesis."

Summer classes had already started, and at least half the tables in the café were taken up by students sitting in front of computers, texting, or both. I had cleaned my own plate, so I reached across the table to start on Darshan's curly fries. "I don't understand how just one fish would get into the pond," I said, dunking a fry into a pool of ketchup.

"That's another good question, Alex," said Dr. Holland. "Discovering the answer will take a lot of research. How would you like to work with our teams?"

A smile spread across my face. I glanced at Darshan, who had stopped chewing. He didn't want to be left out. Besides, the idea of spending so much time with a bunch of adults was much more appealing to me if he were there as well.

"Darshan, too?"

"Of course Darshan, too. I saw how he used that net," said Dr. Holland. He slapped Darshan on the back. "You're a real natural for this kind of work, my boy."

"Thanks," he said, popping a fry in his mouth. "If we find more fish, you can count on me to scoop them up."

"I don't expect to find any in the lake," said Dr. Holland.

"Okay, but what makes you think the fish live underground?" asked Darshan. He slid his plate toward me so I didn't have to reach so far to steal his fries.

"My assumption is based on a couple of important characteristics," he said. "It has no eyes, which leads me to suspect that for millions of years these fish have lived in a place where there's no light. And then there's its color. The pink hue indicates a lack of pigmentation, a common feature of certain cave dwelling creatures."

Just then Dr. Holland's phone rang. My fish had arrived on campus.

CHAPTER 10

The environmental sciences lab consisted of several adjoining rooms with long tables, aquariums and terrariums, microscopes, and various pieces of equipment I couldn't identify. Some of the tanks contained species of plants, algae, or fungi being studied.

The two students who had transported the fish from my house were in the process of setting up a large tank with a filter and aerator. They set a few rocks and plants collected from the edge of the pond into the tank. Octopus Guy wheeled in a dolly that carried one of the barrels of water. More pond or lake water would be collected and stored for use when the aquarium needed it. The staff worked so efficiently that within fifteen minutes the fish was already in its new home—a tank six feet long that imitated the environment of the pond.

Dr. Holland clasped his hands in approval. "Let's hope it'll be happy here."

I pressed my nose against the glass. Darshan tapped his finger on the side, and the fish followed the vibration as if it were stalking a meal. "It looks even weirder from the side," he said.

"That it does," said Dr. Holland. "Viewing it from above when it was in the bathtub made it hard to really appreciate all of its unusual features."

We watched the fish in silence for a long time. Its three dorsal fins cut through the water as it swam, sometimes propelling itself like an ordinary fish, and other times creeping over the rocks with its small, foot-like fins. Its long, thick whiskers shifted continuously as it explored its home from end to end. Not once did it bump into the glass walls or the stones.

The girl from the transport crew placed a thermometer in the tank. "Dr. Holland, I can come in for extra shifts if you need me to babysit the fish," she said.

"I might take you up on that," said Dr. Holland. Then he turned to me and Darshan. "You know, I don't think you were all properly introduced back at the house. This is Carla Ramirez, one of my new students. She's working for me this summer."

We shook hands. At our house I had been so busy looking at Octopus Guy's tattoos that I hadn't really noticed her. Carla was hefty, with broad shoulders, bright smiling eyes, and teeth so straight and white she could be in a toothpaste commercial.

"Carla, why don't you fill them in about what we do here. I'm going to try Dr. Mertz again. I haven't been able to reach him yet." Dr. Holland flipped open his ancient cell phone and dialed as he walked to an adjoining room.

Carla placed a water sample from the tank in front of an electronic device on the lab table. "This is a pH meter," she said. The meter was about the size of a Harry Potter hardcover book and had a retractable arm that could move around like Harry waving his wand. Carla dipped the glass probe at the end of the arm into the sample cup.

"Right now I'm testing the pH level," she said. "That's a measurement of how acidic or alkaline the water is. It helps determine how toxic any present metals and minerals might be to aquatic life."

I remembered learning about that in elementary school, and watching test strips turn red or blue. "We tested pH levels with litmus paper in science class," I said.

"That can give you a rough estimate, but this device is far more accurate. We often use it to check for effects of pollution on water. For instance, chemical waste from factories or mines might make water so acidic that it would be poisonous to both humans and marine life."

Normally I'd be interested in all the details, but right now I was preoccupied with my fish. I stepped back to join Darshan, who hadn't moved from his spot in front of the tank. He had begun a sketch from the new, improved angle, and his eyes bounced back and forth between his spiral sketch pad and the tank like a ping-pong ball.

"Carla, who's going to be taking care of my fish?" I asked.

She cleaned the probe end of the pH tester, tucked in the arm, and covered the machine with a plastic dust hood before taking her place on the other side of Darshan. "The news has spread through the department in just a couple of hours, and everyone wants to be part of the excitement," she said. "This fish is such a prize that Dr. Holland doesn't want to leave it alone for even a minute. Between the department staff, students, and volunteers, I think there will be people watching it day and night, at least for the next few days."

"Shh, listen," said Darshan, putting a finger to his lips. "It sounds like there might be some kind of problem." We could hear Dr. Holland on the phone in the next room.

"Dr. Mertz, I *did* call you right away. Didn't you get my messages?...I'm sorry you had to hear about it from a reporter... No, I have no idea who called the newspaper—it certainly wasn't me...I already told you, I phoned you immediately. Check your voicemail, you'll see."

I whispered to Carla. "Who is this 'Dr. Mertz'?"

She held up a hand to hush me, and cocked her head, straining to hear every word. Clearly, this was important.

43

Dr. Holland continued to argue. He sounded anxious. "I can handle things, I assure you. We're already set up, and I have a hypothesis about…"

I peeked through the doorway. Dr. Holland's back was to me. He was rubbing his forehead and shaking his head.

"Yes, of course, every step of the way," said Dr. Holland. He hung up the phone and heaved a sigh. Then I heard him say a word that, had I used it, would have gotten me in trouble.

CHAPTER 11

"Who's Dr. Mertz?" I asked Dr. Holland when he came back in.

"He's the chairman of the Environmental Sciences Department," said Dr. Holland. "A big man around here. He wants to meet you to congratulate you on this great discovery."

Based on Dr. Holland's tone and exaggerated smile, I had a feeling that congratulating me wasn't Mertz's real motive.

"I have to run over to his office for a few minutes," said Dr. Holland. "I'll be back soon." Again that fake smile. Beneath it he looked nervous, or angry, or both.

When he left the room, I asked Carla about Dr. Mertz.

"He's a 'big man' all right," she said. "Big belly. Big office. Big ego. I've taken a couple of his classes."

"You don't seem to like him," said Darshan.

Carla twisted her face and shrugged. She sat down on the step stool next to the tank. The three of us watched my fish swim back and forth, back and forth, like a caged animal. Well, it *was* a caged animal. "Why do you really think Dr. Mertz wants to meet me?"

"From what I've seen, he doesn't like anyone to get more attention than he does," said Carla. "He's the kind of person who needs to be the bride at every wedding and the corpse at every funeral."

Darshan and I laughed.

"The word around here is that Dr. Mertz has a habit of forcing his way into everyone's research to make sure his name is included on the published papers," she continued. "So if *you're* in the news for this discovery, he needs to latch on somehow."

"Why is that so important to him?" I asked.

Darshan jumped in. "If he doesn't keep publishing new research, he could lose his job as chairman of the department." Because of his parents' jobs, Darshan knew a lot about university politics.

"Yep," said Carla. "It's 'publish or perish' as they say in this field. And from the sound of it, I'm betting he's not very happy that Dr. Holland got to you and the fish first."

"Well, I'm going to tell him that I want Dr. Holland to do the research on my fish, not him," I said defiantly.

"I don't think either you or Dr. Holland will have a say in the matter," said Carla. "Mertz is the boss."

Boss schmoss. I didn't have to meet this man to know I didn't like him. I vowed not to let him ruin our summer.

****

I paced the porch with the phone pressed to my ear. "…and Dr. Holland says it's probably the same species as the Walking Fish fossil, or at least a close relative. The one they thought was extinct. So, *ha!* Who's laughing now, Grandpa?"

For the first time ever, my grandfather was pun-less. I knew that, on the other end of the line, he was examining my emailed photos of the bizarre, eyeless fish.

"Well?" I prodded. "What do you have to say?"

"I'd say your mother is probably already working on a recipe for curried Walking Fish. It'll make her cookbook a best seller."

I plopped onto the porch swing and rocked, the chains squeaking and squawking like a parrot.

"Ha, ha. Seriously, Grandpa, do you think it'll be named after me?"

"I couldn't say. But do you know what they call a fish with no eyes?"

I pressed my feet to the floor to halt the rocking, surprised to learn there was a name for such a fish. "What?"

"*Fsh*," said Grandpa.

"Wha—oh, I get it!" I giggled. "No letter *i*. That's funny, Grandpa. But really, tell me how proud you are of me. Even *you* never caught anything this impressive."

"Very proud indeed," he said. "It's quite the catch. Though I've got to say, my mermaid was prettier."

"Sure she was," I said. "Goodnight, Grandpa."

"Goodnight, Minnow."

****

The next day, Darshan and I hopped into the back of Mr. Mishra's van. It was equipped to drive with hand controls rather than foot pedals. While his parents were at work, Darshan and I would spend the day touring the Environmental Sciences Department, visiting the fish, and—we promised—staying out of trouble.

Darshan pointed to the insulated lunch bag on my lap. "What kind of gourmet lunch did your mom pack for us?"

"Don't worry. She knows you're a vegetarian."

"Okay, then my guess is cheese on a home baked multi-grain roll with tomatoes and pesto sauce. And a side of Dijon potato salad."

"I doubt it," I said, unzipping the bag. "Lately she's been experimenting with quinoa recipes. It's her new favorite 'super food.' So my bet is that it's some sort of grainy salad." I lifted a plastic container from the bag and popped open the lid, releasing a light citrus scent. "I win," I said, thrusting it under Darshan's nose. "On the other hand, being right actually means I *lose*. I'm getting so tired of this stuff."

Darshan sniffed the mix of steamed veggies and mandarin orange slices tossed in the pearly grain. "I think it smells pretty good," he said. "Oh, look, it has almonds and dried cranberries, too. I'll eat yours if you don't want it."

Mr. Mishra stopped the car in front of the two-story brick building. "Here's your stop."

Rather than meeting Dr. Holland in his office, we headed directly to the lab. I was eager to see my fish again.

When we got to the tank, we were shocked by what we found. The fish appeared sluggish and sickly. Its normal pale pink color had taken on a grayish hue. Bags of ice cubes floated in the water. A video camera on a tripod was aimed at the aquarium. Carla sat next to the tank, jotting notes.

"What's wrong with him?" I asked, swallowing my panic.

"Not sure. 'Fishsitters' have been here around the clock, monitoring the temperature, pH, and oxygen levels. We've also been running that camera to record the fish's behavior."

"What did they find?" asked Darshan. He pulled a chair in front of the tank, settling in to watch as if it were a TV screen.

"I've only been here since nine this morning, but the report from Dr. Holland is that the fish took a bad turn during the night. Its color changed, and as you can see, it's kind of wobbly. Instead of swimming, it's been hanging out really close to the filter where the water circulates into the tank."

She pointed out the filtration system. Part of it was suspended in the water, while the electric pump sat beneath the tank. "The overnight shift was sure it was dying. Then Dr. Holland wondered if maybe it was seeking cooler water. If he's right about it living in a cave, that would make sense, right? So he placed bags of ice into the water to gradually lower the temperature. When it reached about fifty-two degrees Fahrenheit, the fish did seem to improve a bit."

"Isn't the water just going to warm right back up to room temperature after the ice melts?" Darshan asked.

Carla nodded. "Dr. Holland put in a rush order for an aquarium chiller to keep the temperature at a constant level. It's being shipped by overnight mail so it should get here tomorrow. In the meantime, we keep adding bags of ice and monitoring the temperature to keep it at fifty-two."

The knot in my stomach tightened. I tapped on the tank. The fish fluttered its fins and wriggled a bit, but a moment later became still again. The little dimple behind its head pulsated in time with its gills.

"Is he going to die?" I asked, my voice cracking.

Carla crinkled her brow. "Let's hope not. Dr. Holland should be here in a few minutes. He can tell you more."

Soon Dr. Holland strolled in wearing the same clothes as the day before—wrinkled khakis and a crumpled, short sleeve button-down shirt. His graying hair poked up on one side. It was clear that he had been up with the fish all night.

"Hello, ladies and gents!" His cheeriness was clearly forced.

"Hi, Dr. H," I said weakly. "Please tell me my fish is going to live."

"I wish I could promise you that. We're doing everything we can." Then he addressed Carla. "I don't know what I was thinking. We set up the tank to imitate Glacial Lake and the pond, when we obviously should have been going for a cave environment. First of all, plants don't grow deep in a cave, so there shouldn't be any in the tank."

"Right." Without a moment's delay, she plunged a net into the water, scooped out a plant and dropped it into a bucket.

Dr. Holland took the net from her and set it in the bucket with the plant. "Don't bother. We're relocating the fish. Come with me."

He led us down the hall to a spacious room, dimly lit with black light lamps. Tanks and cages lined the walls, each containing small nocturnal animals, from bats, to catfish, to cockroaches. According to Dr. Holland, students were studying the impact of various environmental changes on all the creatures.

A new tank already awaited my fish, its filter humming and aerator bubbling. Octopus Guy, whose real name I never did catch, nodded to us in greeting as he arranged stones beneath the murky pond water. He had piled a few at the bottom to create a little hill. A couple of gallon-sized Ziploc bags of ice floated at the top.

"We'll wait until the water in this new tank is exactly the same temperature as the fish's current tank," said Dr. Holland. "Then we'll transfer our friend to its new pad."

"Its what?" asked Darshan.

"Its new digs."

Darshan, Carla and I stared at him quizzically.

Dr. Holland threw up his hands. "Its new *home*. We'll move it to its new home." Then he murmured to himself. "I keep forgetting these kids were, in fact, born yesterday."

As Dr. Holland instructed Carla and Octopus Guy, Darshan and I wandered around the room. In one tank, a litter of tiny pink newborn mice, with a layer of skin still covering their eyes, nursed their mother. They looked to me like little grubs.

Moving on to a tall screened enclosure built into one corner, I said, "Oh, look Dar—Batman had babies!" A little cluster of bats clung upside down from a tree branch.

Darshan stiffened a little and moved quickly past me to peer into another tank. I joined him to see what was inside. Fireflies flitted among the greenery, blinking their neon light. Upon closer inspection, we discovered that even the larvae, squiggling amidst the damp leaves, lit up an iridescent green.

"Cool," said Darshan. "I never knew that the larvae glow, too."

Neither had I, though I'd never actually thought about it. If I fed one to my fish, would it light up as well? I could only hope that, whatever they fed my fish, the team of professors and students could get it back to looking as healthy as the other critters in here.

We returned to the room with the Walking Fish, who sure wasn't doing any walking now. Or swimming, for that matter. Dr. Holland opened a plastic container and held it out to me. "Want to feed him?"

"What is it?" I asked. Bug-like creatures darted about in the tub of water. I took a closer look. "Hey, aren't those sea monkeys? I had some of those when I was little."

Dr. Holland snorted. "There's no such thing as sea monkeys. Some clever dude made up the cute name to sell plain old brine shrimp as exotic pets. Anyway, we're not sure what our fish eats, but small shrimp are found in the cave waters around here,

51

and some other cave fish species do feed on them, so it's a reasonable guess."

I poured half the container into the tank. Dozens of the grey critters spread out, hanging in mid water, huddling in corners, and settling near rocks. My fish's whiskers moved a little, and I hoped it might sense the meal nearby. It did not. I poured in the rest of the shrimp.

"Listen up," said Dr. Holland. "We're going to do what we can to save Alex's fish, but in order to search for more of them, we need help beyond the university. I've called the OER—that's the Office of Environmental Research—and asked them for a marine research boat to study Glacial Lake. We still aren't sure how deep it really is, so besides taking water samples, we'll be checking into that, too. I've also put in a call for divers. Some of our students are scuba trained and have volunteered their skills."

Perhaps the bottom of the lake would yield some answers.

CHAPTER 12

It took barely an instant to confirm my dislike of Dr. Mertz. Perhaps it was the way he talked down to me, or the way he interrupted when Dr. Holland was talking. And I was pretty sure he was flirting with my mother.

My parents invited both professors over for lunch when they learned Dr. Mertz wanted to meet me. But Dr. Mertz didn't really seem interested in me at all. Mom, Dad and Dr. Holland sat in a row on the couch, in polite attention. Dr. Mertz rattled on about himself and his research. It was clear he wanted my parents to know how very important he was. You'd think he was talking to himself, the way his eyes focused anywhere but on the person he was supposedly addressing. My father always says, "Don't trust anyone who won't look you in the eye." That was one more reason I didn't trust this man.

The most annoying thing about him, I decided, was how he wandered around the room as he chattered, picking up random objects, studying them, and placing them down again. He examined a Navajo vase on the fireplace mantle like he was searching for a price tag. He flipped through the *National Geographic* magazine and then tossed it down so haphazardly that it slid off the coffee table onto the floor. He picked up my dad's car keys from the carved bowl near the door and jingled them before dropping them back in. Dad fixed his eyes on the man, as if to make sure nothing ended up in Mertz's pockets. Of course, maybe Dad was actually interested in what he was saying. It's hard to tell with those science types.

Darshan ignored it all, and instead busied himself drawing a cartoon of Dr. Mertz on his napkin.

When I saw what the professor reached for next, I clutched Darshan's wrist, sending the pencil flying from his hand. "Oh, please, no!" I said in a high-pitched whisper. "Tell me I'm imagining!"

As Mertz babbled about some award he had won, he lifted my dental retainer from a glass dish on the dining table and stroked it mindlessly with his thumb, as if it were a pet mouse.

I cringed. "Ick!" The other adults in the room hid their disgust better, though I could see it in their eyes and downturned lips.

Darshan wagged his finger at me in mock scolding and whispered, "It's your own fault for not having it in your mouth where it belongs."

Dr. Mertz dropped the retainer back in the dish. The moment he turned his back I snatched it up, bolted to the kitchen, and tossed it into the dishwasher. When I returned to the table, he still hadn't paused long enough to take a breath.

On and on Dr. Mertz babbled. My mother wore a frozen smile, though her eyes had glazed over. Dr. Holland glanced at his watch. My dad was the only one who seemed to still be interested, unless he just faked it better than anyone else. Eventually I let my mind wander and found myself studying the chipped nail on my right pinky finger. I chewed on it until Darshan poked me in the side with his pencil eraser. He gestured with his chin toward Mertz.

"Watch his face."

While talking about leading the fish research, the professor had become so excited that his chubby face now glowed a rosy red. A large blue vein had appeared on his forehead, running up from the bridge of his nose to his receding hairline. His bushy white mustache wiggled up and down as he spoke.

"He's red, white and blue!" Darshan whispered.

"Yep, just like Old Glory, the American flag," I giggled. With Mertz's back to me, I stood at attention and raised my right hand to my head in a salute.

Mom gave us a stern look. "Did you hear what Dr. Mertz just said?" she asked. "He would like you to consider giving your fish to the university as a gift. It would belong to the Environmental Sciences Department and they could study it however they see fit."

So *that's* what this meeting was really about.

"Can't they study it even if it stays my fish?" I asked.

"It would complicate things unless it officially belongs to us," said Dr. Mertz. "It would be much simpler if you gift it to the school."

He drew an envelope from inside his blazer, drew out a document, and laid it on the dining room table. He placed a pen next to it, and for the first time, really looked at me.

I didn't move.

"There will be a very nice plaque thanking you," he added with a wink. Then holding his thumbs and forefingers up to form a frame, he recited, "With gratitude to Alexis Byron for her generous gift of the Walking Fish."

I looked beyond him. Dr. Holland's expression was sort of blank and hard to read, like he was struggling to keep his mouth shut when he had something to say.

"Dr. H, I thought you said it would be called the Alex Fish."

Mertz didn't give Dr. Holland a chance to answer. "Alex Fish, Walking Fish, does it really matter? At this point we do suspect it's the Walking Fish, though we have only a single fossil for

55

comparison. It could be a close relative. But no matter what it's called, you've made an important discovery, young lady." For a fleeting moment, he seemed sincere.

Still, if my fish was a living specimen of some ancient species that no one had ever before seen, why should I settle for a stupid plaque? Dr. Holland had promised I could participate in the research. If I gave up all claims to the fish, Old Glory could prevent my involvement. If that was his plan, it was a deal breaker.

"If I give you the fish, can I help in the search for more fish, and in the research?" I asked. Then I felt an elbow in my side. "Oh, and Darshan, too."

Mertz gave me the kind of sugary-sweet smile usually reserved for cute babies. "My dear, why don't you leave that for the scientists? It's grown-up work." Then he wove his fingers together and gazed skyward, as if in deep contemplation. His face brightened and he said enthusiastically, "Tell you what; I will personally give both you and your friend a weekly briefing on everything we do. I won't leave out a thing." It was like wrestling a juicy bone from a puppy and replacing it with a piece of wilted lettuce.

"No thanks," I said, shaking my head. "I think I want my fish back."

His red face went pale. In a low voice through gritted teeth he asked, "Now, what would you do with the fish? You don't even have a tank to keep it in."

I tilted my head and smiled sweetly. "My Grandpa can mount it. It will look great on the wall over our fireplace."

Mertz went from pale to white. My parents stared at me wide-eyed. One corner of Dr. Holland's lips curled upward.

Darshan pretended to cough into the napkin he'd been doodling on in order to stifle a laugh. His sketch of Dr. Mertz, adorned in stars and stripes, was now damp with spit.

Mertz shot a glance at my parents. He obviously hoped for help in controlling their disrespectful child.

My father rubbed his chin. "You heard her terms, Dr. Mertz. What'll it be?"

A tense silence followed. Finally Dr. Mertz ran a trembling hand through his thin hair. "Oh heck, sure you can help. It'll be great to have a smart young lady like you involved with the studies." His lips stretched into a tight smile, though anger flashed behind his eyes.

With that settled, we discussed the governor's visit the next day. He would be taken to see the fish at Glacial Lake University first thing in the morning. "After a stop at GLU, he'll be coming here to meet you, Alexis, and to view the pond where you caught the fish," said Dr. Mertz. "There will be reporters, but don't let that make you nervous—I'll do all the talking."

Of course you will, I thought. Truth is, I wasn't interested enough in the governor's visit to be nervous. I'm not particularly interested in politics or politicians, and was eager to get started on fun science stuff.

"We'd better spruce up the place," said Mom. She sprang from the couch and began to organize the magazines on the end table. "I wonder," she said, bolting upright, "what does one wear to meet the governor?"

I glimpsed down at my own attire. "Shorts and t-shirt, I hope. That's all I packed for the summer." I turned to Darshan. "Dar, what are you going to wear?"

Mertz interrupted. "I think we'll be keeping this a small, intimate meeting."

"Perfect," I said. "I'm small. And Darshan is my closest friend, so he's intimate."

Dr. Mertz's mustache twitched as he eyed Darshan. A little growl rose from his throat. "All right, then. I hear that the two of you caught the fish together, so it would be appropriate for you both to be there. But this gathering will be restricted to you two kids, Alexis's parents, and me."

Dr. Holland glared at Dr. Mertz from across the room, his jaws clenched. This wasn't fair.

"Don't you think Dr. Holland should come, too?" I asked, knowing I was close to crossing the line.

Dr. Holland quickly jumped in. "Never mind, Alex. You heard the chairman. You can tell me all about it later."

CHAPTER 13

From my upside-down position on the porch swing, I pushed myself off the wall with my feet, letting my hair drag back and forth across the floorboards. I had fastened the phone to the side of my head with an elastic headband, leaving my hands free, though there was no one out here to see my gestures.

"So then, Old Glory actually picks up my retainer with his disgusting sausage fingers and *plays* with it. I swear, Grandpa, I'd rather have crooked teeth for the rest of my life than to ever put that retainer in my mouth again."

"Why wasn't it in your mouth where it belongs?"

"Focus, Grandpa. We're talking about my fish."

"No, you pretty much veered off that topic and onto sausages and crooked teeth."

"Ugh, never mind that. But you should have seen Old Glory's face when I told him you would mount the fish on the wall for me." My upside-down laughter sounded like a snorting piglet.

"Mount it?" Grandpa said in a horrified tone. "Why, I'd never do such a thing."

"You wouldn't?" His response surprised me, since his biggest swordfish was mounted over his own fireplace.

"Heck, no. I'd cook it up with a nice white wine sauce and a pinch of tarragon."

I flipped myself upright and crossed my legs on the swing. "Grandpa, do you think I made a mistake giving him the Walking Fish? After all, it's *my* fish. Why should the university own it?"

Grandpa drew in a long, deep breath. *Wait for it*, I thought. Would he answer with a pun or a riddle?

"Minnow, did I ever tell you about the time I went fishing with my father? I was about your age, and hooked the biggest catch ever."

I groaned. "Please, no more mermaid stories."

"Not a mermaid," Grandpa corrected in an unusually serious tone, "A tuna. Huge and powerful. Back then, even with a full set of fingers, I couldn't have weighed more than ninety pounds."

"You were petite like me?" I asked.

Grandpa scoffed. "No, I was *not* petite. I prefer the term 'compact.' Let's just say, in a boxing ring I would have been in the flyweight category. Anyway, my fishing pole was bowed practically in two by the weight of the tuna. My old man—the greatest fisherman I ever knew—saw me struggling and tried to help me bring that big fish in. I refused to let him take the pole. It was *my* fish, and if he helped, that would make it his fish, too. I needed to prove myself, and wasn't about to share my prize or the glory of the catch. So Pop backed off and watched. In the end, I wore out before the fish did, and let the line go slack. At that moment, the tuna leapt from the water and broke the line. My fish got away, and I went home empty handed."

I understood. "I get it. You're saying that by giving my fish to the university, everybody wins."

"Oh, I don't know about that. What I was going to say is that, instead of tuna steaks for dinner, we had my mother's famous meatloaf. And all it was famous for was indigestion."

And there it was.

"Thanks for the wise words," I said. "Goodnight, Grandpa."

"Goodnight, Minnow."

****

That night I dreamed that I was swimming with a school of Walking Fish and was caught in a net by none other than Dr. Mertz. When he brought me to his lab for research, I tried to scream, "I'm a girl, not a fish!" but no sound came out. I awoke with my heart pounding and pajama top drenched in sweat. The soft light of early dawn filtered through my window. There was no way I'd get back to sleep. My parents were still in bed, so I dressed quietly. I decided to take a walk to the pond and lake. Maybe the dream was a premonition that I would find another fish. If I did catch another, it would be for Dr. Holland. I would not give it to Old Glory.

It would be easy to check the pond and the near side of the lake, and still be home in time for breakfast. *Can't meet the Governor on an empty stomach,* I thought. So I jotted a note for my parents—"Gone fishing"—and was out the door by 6:30, with a bucket and net in case I got lucky. By 7:00 I had rechecked both of the ponds near the cabin, poking around stones with the handle of the net. If there were any more fish in there, they were keeping well out of sight.

Curiously, the smaller pond seemed significantly smaller than it was the day we arrived, while the larger pond, where I had discovered my fish, was shrinking much more gradually. I studied the surrounding mountains and trees to assess whether one pond might be getting more sun than the other. That might account for a difference in evaporation. Yet I concluded that, if anything, the smaller pond was a bit shadier.

I strolled along the lake edge, and by 8:30 I had covered about a half mile of the shore.

"Hey kid, what are you doing here?" someone yelled.

I squinted against the sun to see who had spoken. "I'm hunting for fish," I called back.

A policeman made his way toward me from the road, shuffling down the steep embankment and probably scuffing up his shiny black shoes.

"How did you get down here?" he asked. "This whole area is closed till noon because of the governor's visit. Didn't you see the barricades on the road?"

"I didn't come from the road," I said.

"Well, regardless of however you got here, I'll have to ask you to leave," he said flatly.

I started to head back home the way I came, by way of the lakeshore.

"I'm sorry, you can't go that way," said the policeman. "No one is allowed around the lake. You have to go up to the road."

"But Officer, my house is that way." I pointed in the direction of my cabin.

He huffed with impatience, arms crossed over his chest. "What part of 'not allowed' don't you understand?" He meant business.

I could have kicked myself for not taking my mother's cell phone, and I was too afraid of the surly policeman to ask if I could use his to call my parents. So, with my bucket and net, I headed up the embankment to the road. Now and then, I checked to see if he was still there, so that I might sneak back down and make a run for home. But he had stationed himself on a boulder where he had a clear view of the lake and shoreline in all directions. And he kept his eye on me.

When I reached the road, I found myself next to the officer's patrol car. At least I assumed it was his, since there was no one else in or near the car. Its lights were flashing.

I looked left, the direction that would take me home. A second cruiser was parked sideways to block the street, just behind a barricade with a detour sign. A policeman reclined against the car. He was texting or something, paying no attention to me. I figured that, like the other officer, he would refuse to let me through.

That's when I got an idea. I set the fishing net and bucket on the back of the officer's car. As he watched me suspiciously from below, I slid my finger around on the dusty trunk. *ALEXIS BYRON WENT THAT WAY,* I wrote, with an arrow pointing into town. Then I skipped toward Glacial Village.

CHAPTER 14

I guessed that by now it was close to nine and I knew my parents would begin to worry. At least I had left them a note. If they went searching for me, they'd probably run into the policeman who would tell them what had happened.

I ran till I became winded, walked till I caught my breath, and ran some more. I hadn't realized how far the village was from my house. It only seemed like a few minutes on my bike, and no time at all in the car.

The main road into town did look familiar. I knew that one of the side streets led to the Hollands' house where my parents and I had visited several times. I read each street sign I passed, but I wasn't certain I'd recognize the name even if I saw it.

Two workmen were busy filling in a pothole on the road. One was tall, thin, and bearded, and resembled a young Abe Lincoln. The other was stocky with curly dark hair. They waved a friendly hello.

"Hi," I greeted. "I'm looking for Dr. Holland's house. He works at the university. I know he lives somewhere along this road, but I don't know the street."

Abe Lincoln stroked his scraggly whiskers. Curly shook his head apologetically.

"He's the professor who identified the prehistoric fish," I added. "It was reported on the local radio channel yesterday. Soon it'll be all over the news."

"Oh yeah, I heard about that fish," said Abe. "Though the name I heard was *Mertz*, not Holland. And some kid named Brian."

"Mertz is a phony," I sneered. "And it's *Byron*, not *Brian*."

"Sorry, can't help you, kid," said Curly. He leaned his shovel against the guardrail. "Here, you want to use my phone?"

I considered calling my parents. Then I noticed the wildflowers on the side of the road.

"You might know Dr. Holland's house by his wife's famous garden. It was in *Home and Garden Magazine*."

"Oh, sure, everybody knows *that* place," said Abe. "My wife made me drive by there last month. Now she wants me to rip up our front lawn and put in a bunch of rose bushes." He chuckled. "Anyway, you're really close. Make a right at that stop sign, and it's about two blocks down. You can't miss it."

I could see the burst of colors from the famous garden a block away, and smelled the flowers a half a block before reaching them. An arbor arched over the front gate, exploding with climbing roses. I opened the gate and entered the front yard. More roses in pink, red, yellow and white lined the fieldstone walkway leading up to the house. Towering sunflowers, as tall as my dad, lined either side of the front steps.

I paused briefly at the little pond in front of the house. Yellow lilies bloomed on the floating green lily pads. Several spotted koi darted to the surface when I approached the edge of the pond.

"Sorry, fishies, I don't have any food for you." I wondered why these fish hadn't been eaten by herons or raccoons like the fish in Darshan's pond. Just then, a sleek Siamese cat shot off the Hollands' porch to chase a crow, and I knew the answer.

I sprinted up the steps where a second cat, pure white with a triangle of grey between its eyes, lazily swayed its tail. When a lizard scurried right in front of its feet—a dream come true for most felines—this cat yawned and closed its eyes. The birds in the yard sure didn't have to worry about this one.

Through glass panes beside the front door I saw the grandfather clock in the foyer. It was now nine-thirty, only half an hour before the governor was scheduled to arrive. I rang the bell, and in a moment Mrs. Holland was at the door with pancake batter on her nose. Dr. Holland stood behind her in the foyer. He wore blue jeans with a dishrag hanging from the waistband, and a Glacial Lake Music Festival t-shirt. He, too, had batter on his nose. I couldn't help but wonder what the two of them had been up to. A food fight?

"My, what a surprise! What on earth are you doing here this morning?" asked Mrs. Holland. She craned her neck to look up and down the street. "Where are your parents?"

As sweat dripped down my neck, I told them about my encounter with the policeman at the lake, the detours on the road, and how I found my way to their home.

"Well, come in and have something cold to drink. We can call your folks to pick you up," said Mrs. Holland.

"No, no," I answered, a little too emphatically. "They're really busy getting ready for the governor's visit. Can you drive me back to my house, Dr. H?"

"Of course I will," he replied. He glanced at the face of the grandfather clock. "We'd better skedaddle if we have to take all of the back roads to avoid the roadblocks." He grabbed his pipe and car keys from a table near the door.

"Thanks," I said. "Mrs. H, would you please call my parents for me and tell them that I'm on my way home?"

"Absolutely." She kissed my cheek and waved as we left.

Dr. Holland and I hopped into his rusted old van. Its sides and fenders were plastered with old, faded bumper stickers: *Impeach Nixon. Make Love, Not War. Vote for Equal Rights.*

The engine stalled when Dr. Holland first turned the key. "Not again," he groaned. "We might have to take my wife's car if it won't—"

Vroooom. On the second try, the car started and we headed along the bumpy back roads to my family's cabin. There wasn't much time.

CHAPTER 15

The old Volkswagen sputtered and rumbled but kept a steady pace.

"I normally drive my wife's Prius for long distances," said Dr. Holland. "It gets great mileage and is better for the environment, but I do love my groovy old van." It was easy to see why my father always teases the professor that he's stuck in the 1960s.

I thumbed through a box of music tapes resting on the floor. I didn't recognize any of the musical groups. "Where are your CDs?" I asked.

"CDs? Do you see a CD player in here? This baby,"—he patted the dashboard lovingly—"she's a classic. Way older than you. Pick out a tape and you'll hear some *real* music."

I chose an unlabeled mix and popped it into the tape deck. Voices sang out in harmony. *"...California dreamin' on such a winter's day...."*

I settled back in my seat, which was covered with some sort of fake fur. "Dr. H, how is my fish doing?"

"I'm not going to lie to you, dear. I don't like the way it's looking. Not moving much, but it's hanging on. If we can figure out where it came from we might find others like it. That way, if it…" He didn't finish his sentence.

I sighed heavily and stared out the window. Dr. Holland hummed out of tune to a song I never heard of. *"You are the dancing queen, young and sweet…"* All the while, he chewed on his pipe, now and then flipping it with his tongue from one side of his mouth to the other.

"Do you ever light that thing?" I asked.

"Heck no," he said, as if my question were totally insane. "Smoking will kill you."

When we reached a police barricade near my street, Dr. Holland stuck his head out the window and shouted, "Hey, I'm the chauffeur for Miss Alexis Byron. That's *the* Miss Alexis Byron. The governor is waiting to meet her."

The officer stuck his head in the window and eyed me suspiciously. "You're the Byron girl?" I nodded. I giggled as he moved the barricade to let us through.

We passed a line of cars and news vehicles parked along the road, their occupants milling around drinking from paper Starbucks cups. Dr. Mertz's BMW was in our driveway. Dr. Holland had to find a spot farther down the street in front of Darshan's house. The moment we parked, I bolted from the car and sprinted toward my house, with Dr. Holland following close behind.

My mother waited anxiously on the front porch with the local police chief. "You had us worried sick. Why didn't you take my phone when you left? Oh, never mind. Chief Collins went out to look for you and found your message on that policeman's car." Mom let out a nervous little laugh. "I've got to say, that was awfully clever of you. But, oh, that poor officer was so embarrassed when he had to tell Chief Collins how he sent you away. No matter. By then Mrs. Holland had called, thank goodness. David! Good morning! Thanks for bringing Alex home. Did you have anything to eat? I can whip you up some boysenberry waffles in no time at all."

"Mom, take a chill pill, will you!" I said. She gets all weird and hyper like this when she's nervous. "We don't have time to eat. The governor will be here any second."

"Oh, right," she said, stretching to see down the street. "That's okay. We have snacks on the back porch anyway."

"You all go ahead," said Chief Collins. "I'll wait out front for the governor and escort him back."

Dr. Mertz didn't see Dr. Holland and me enter the yard. He stood on the back porch with my dad, popping mini quiches and strawberry scones into his mouth one after another. Even from a few yards away I could see crumbs cling to his mustache, and powdered sugar dusting his tie.

"We should go say hello, and let him know why I'm here uninvited," said Dr. Holland. Before we could do so, Chief Collins escorted the governor into the yard, followed by a horde of reporters that swarmed around him like bees around a hive.

"Too late. We probably shouldn't keep 'the Gov' waiting, right?" I said. I took Dr. Holland's arm and we strolled together toward the crowd.

"There she is!" someone shouted. The reporters separated to make room for Dr. Holland and me. Cameras were rolling.

The governor extended his hand to me. "Congratulations, young lady. This is quite an accomplishment for someone your age. For someone any age, really."

"Thank you, sir," I said. "Oh, this here is Dr. Holland from the Environmental Sciences Department at GLU. He's the *very first* professor to see my fish and get it to the university."

I nudged Dr. Holland with my shoulder. "Tell them your ideas about how we'll find out how it got here and where it came from."

The reporters stuck microphones in Dr. Holland's face, allowing me to slip away and join Darshan and my parents near the porch.

"Where's Old Glory? I asked. "Last I saw he was up there stuffing his face at the snack table."

"Alexis, show some respect," my mother scolded.

Darshan pointed toward the side of the yard. "Now he's doing it down there, all by himself."

Dr. Mertz stood grimly like a garden gnome in the shade of a mossy oak, stubbornly refusing to join the others. He had obviously hoped to be the center of attention, chatting up the governor and pointing out the pond where the amazing fish was found. Things weren't going quite that way, and it looked like his pride was keeping him from competing with Dr. Holland. He reached into a bulging jacket pocket and popped something in his mouth. I was astounded to realize that he had filled his pocket with pastries. It was kind of pathetic, really.

"You should have seen his face when he first saw you and Dr. Holland arrive," Darshan said. He held up a napkin on which he had sketched a cartoon of Dr. Mertz with eyes springing on coils from his head. "He looked just like this. I won't repeat what he said, but I was standing right next to him, and I assure you it wasn't very nice."

Even from this distance, Darshan and I could clearly see the blue vein pop through the flushed redness of his forehead, and that white mustache wiggle above his tight lips as he furiously chewed his bounty.

Then, as if scripted, Old Glory raised his hand to his forehead to shade his eyes from the sun. "Look, he's saluting!" I said. We burst out laughing.

"Why are you two giggling like that?" asked my mom. She was sitting with my dad on the porch steps.

"Huh? What?" I raised my eyebrows to put on my best innocent face, and quickly changed the subject. "Hey, don't they look like old friends?" The governor's hand was on Dr. Holland's shoulder and the two were engaged in an animated conversation. Dr. Mertz, probably fed up with being ignored, was shoving his way through the crowd of reporters.

71

My mother's eyes narrowed. "Heeey…" she said. She drew out the word and wagged her finger accusingly. "I bet I know why you asked Dr. Holland to bring you home rather than calling me or your father to pick you up."

"Huh? What?" I seemed to be saying that a lot today. This time, I tried to muster up my best 'confused' expression.

Dad slapped his leg. "Oh, I get it! You needed an excuse to get him here uninvited. What a scheme!"

"Me? You think I did that?" I asked. Should I try my surprised face, innocent face, or angry face? I defaulted to my wide puppy eyes.

"Enough with the innocent act," laughed my father. "It was brilliant."

The governor and the two professors made their way over to me, followed by the gaggle of reporters with cameras. *Click, click, click.*

"There you are," said the governor. "We wondered where you ran off to. Dr. Holland tells me you nearly didn't make it here this morning."

"Yes, sir, but I did, thanks to him. Always the one to save the day."

"So I hear," said the governor.

"Tell us how you caught this extraordinary fish," said one of the reporters. Microphones were aimed at me like little canons. I looked straight into the cameras.

"Well, I have my grandpa to thank, really. It all started one day when he was cutting down a dead maple tree and chopped off four of his favorite fingers…"

CHAPTER 16

That evening, the local station and many of the national stations carried the story of the prehistoric fish discovered by Yours Truly. Experts speculated whether it truly was the prehistoric Walking Fish, and where it might have come from. They commented on the importance of this discovery. Dr. Holland discussed the studies that would need to be done to search for the source of the fish and confirm the species.

"I thought we would see a ten- or fifteen-second news clip, but it got some pretty extensive coverage," said Dad.

"Yeah, but by the time Old Glory got anywhere near the reporters, Dr. H had already said most of what the news people wanted to know," I said, rummaging in the refrigerator for a snack. It was only a half hour past dinner, but I was already hungry again. "Ooh, Mom made triple-cherry cobbler!"

"Alexis," sighed my father, shaking his head, "you have to stop calling Dr. Mertz 'Old Glory.' It's disrespectful."

"Hmmph," I sneered, plopping into a chair with an overflowing bowl of cobbler. "You should hear what I'd really like to call him. Did you notice that when he finally got to meet the governor, he just *had* to mention that he's the one in charge of everything?"

My mother clicked off the TV and picked up a magazine. "It is what it is. Besides, he *is* the department chairman, so what do you expect?" She peered at me over her reading glasses. "I do wish you had at least combed your hair before the interview. You had a great presence on camera, but you looked like a rag doll."

"Hey, I discovered an old fish, not a new hair product. I think I looked perfect for the role." I smoothed my hair down, but wasn't thinking about bad hair days. My mind was on tomorrow's underwater exploration.

Divers arrived early the next morning to search the lake. Park officials prohibited boating during this time, and for the next week or so, swimming would be restricted to a few designated areas.

I put on my favorite swim suit—a yellow bikini with a jumping blue dolphin on one butt cheek. Darshan was waiting on my back porch with a mask and snorkel set in each hand.

"A few divers already went in before I got here," he said. He pointed out three others in wetsuits at the dock, putting on their air tanks. "Those guys are going further out by boat, but they left us this stuff." He handed me one of the snorkeling sets.

Lacking scuba training, Darshan and I were not allowed to join the divers in the deep water. Instead, it was our job was to investigate the pond and the shallower waters around the shore.

We decided to begin with the ever-shrinking ponds. It was still early and both the air and water were chilly.

"Ready?" I asked. With the snorkel already in his mouth, Darshan nodded.

We started in the smaller of the two ponds. We were able to search it pretty quickly, and within minutes went into the bigger pond. Goose bumps broke out on my arms and legs when I immersed myself in the cold water.

Through the mask I could see the bottom of the pond. Weeds and grass had rotted and gone brown beneath the water, and there were lots of the same beige and gray rocks that dotted the yard and shore line. It was definitely not like the gorgeous coral reefs

I'd seen in pictures. No Nemo or Dory or Little Mermaid here. No Walking Fish, either. Nothing at all.

I stood up in the middle of the pond and pushed the mask on top of my head. The water reached the middle of my thigh. Darshan swam toward me, still face down searching for fish. His snorkel protruded like a submarine telescope. I cupped my hand over the hole, making him shoot up in a panic.

"Hey!" he cried. He gave me a playful shove, sending me splashing backward.

I floated on my back. "Have you noticed that this pond is colder than the little one?" I asked. "Especially at that end near the boulder."

"It's deeper. The sun can't warm it as easily." He sank low with only his head poking out, looking like a beach ball with eyes floating on the water. "I didn't see anything under there, did you?"

"Nada," I said. "Want to try the lake? We can snorkel near the shore."

We were knee-deep in the lake when two divers surfaced in the distance. On their backs they paddled closer and closer until the water was shallow enough for them to wade the rest of the way to shore. They resembled aliens emerging from the depths, covered head to foot in hooded black suits with tubes in their mouths.

"Find anything?" I shouted.

The taller diver made a thumbs-down sign before removing the breathing device from his mouth. Then he lifted his mask, revealing the greenest eyes I'd ever seen.

"We're more likely to find life in my toilet bowl than we are down there," he said in an awesome, silky accent. When he stepped onto the beach, he released three buckles across his torso and slipped off the scuba equipment. Standing before us in his sleek, skin-tight diving suit and hood, he looked like a superhero. *Scubaman.*

I sank bashfully into the water, feeling exposed in my bikini. "Oh, hi," I squeaked.

"You're Alexis, aren't you?" he asked. "I'm Gadi." All I could do was nod like a dimwit. Gadi turned to his scuba partner. "Joelle, meet the famous Alexis Byron. She's the one responsible for all this excitement. And this must be Darshan, her able partner." He reached out to shake Darshan's hand.

"Hey," Darshan said. His eyeballs practically popped out of his head as Joelle peeled her dive suit down to her waist, revealing a neon-yellow swimsuit with purple flowers. She snapped off her hood and squeezed water from her long blond hair.

"Nice to meet you kids," Joelle said warmly. She slung the vest with its attached air tank over one shoulder and her fins over the other. The bulky equipment appeared to weigh as much as she did.

Darshan's eyes darted between Joelle and his own knobby knees.

I watched him watching Joelle.

"What?" he snapped when he saw me glaring at him.

Gadi said, "Well, kids, we have to unload this gear and check in with Dr. Mertz. See you later!" We watched silently as they hauled their stuff to the Jeep parked on the narrow gravel road leading to the boat dock.

"Gawd, Darshan, could you be more obvious the way you were gawking at Joelle?" I marched from the beach.

"Who was gawking? I wasn't gawking." He trudged after me. "Plus, you're sure one to talk, the way you were drooling over that Gadi guy."

"Was not!"

"Were so!"

I dropped to the ground near the big pond and stared up at the clouds. Darshan settled a few feet from me, tossing pebbles into the water.

"What does it matter, anyway?" I grumbled. "They called us 'kids.'"

"Yeah," agreed Darshan, and his well-aimed pebble bounced off my ear.

CHAPTER 17

A few days later I waited and watched impatiently at the kitchen window.

"Come have some breakfast," said my mother.

I didn't budge.

"Hey!" My mother snapped her fingers to get my attention. "They'll get here when they get here, and you need to put something in your stomach before you go up."

I practically inhaled my breakfast (Hawaiian pancakes stuffed with fresh pineapple and coconut), and soon heard the rattle of a pickup truck as it turned onto the dock access road. The gravel crunched beneath the tires.

I gulped down the last of my hot choco-mint cocoa (Godiva chocolate melted in low fat milk, simmered with fresh garden mint), and bolted for the back door.

As usual, Darshan was already waiting outside. Even though there would not be room for us both on the boat, he wasn't about to miss seeing it launch with all its fancy equipment. He waved his arms wildly at me as I raced down to the water.

When the truck came to a stop near the dock, two OER agents stepped out and began to unload their gear from the back of the vehicle.

Out of breath, I panted, "Hi, I'm Alex…and this…is Darshan."

"You didn't have to run," one of the agents said. She was a tall, freckle-faced woman in her thirties. Even her lips had freckles. "We're a few minutes early, but we do need to get started on time. I'm Julia," she said, extending her freckled hand to me. "This here is Eli."

"Where is the boat?" I asked. "Is it coming on another truck?"

"You're standing next to it," said Julia.

Darshan and I stared blankly at the bundle attached by a hose to a large cylinder. "I don't see any boat," I said.

"Want to see a trick?" asked Eli. "In a moment a boat will miraculously appear with a wave of my wand." He twisted a knob on the cylinder and theatrically waved an imaginary wand in front of the bundle.

It was, in fact, like magic. With a loud "whoosh," the package began to unfold and take shape. It grew and grew, and in a few short minutes we stood beside a rubber boat, large enough for five people. Eli and Julia carried it to the dock. The two were still loading it with the research equipment from the truck when Dr. Holland arrived.

"Hey folks," he said. He looked around. "Where's Dr. Mertz?"

"Not here yet," I said.

By this time my mom had appeared at the dock with a thermos and a stack of Styrofoam cups. "Choco-mint cocoa, anyone?"

"Thanks, it sounds delish, but I don't think we have time," Julia said. "We need to leave in a few minutes. Maybe someone should call Dr. Mertz to see where he is."

Dr. Holland called and got his voicemail. What a surprise.

When Dr. Mertz still hadn't shown up twenty minutes later, Eli said, "We only have the boat and equipment for four hours. In five minutes, we either leave without him or cancel altogether."

Dr. Holland sighed deeply. "He won't be happy if we go without him, but cancelling is *not* an option." He mumbled under his breath, "Why doesn't that man ever answer his calls?"

I tugged his sleeve eagerly. "If Old Glory—I mean, if Dr. Mertz doesn't make it, can Darshan take his place on the boat?"

"Oh, yeah! Can I?" Darshan looked pleadingly at Dr. Holland. His dark, hound dog eyes were way harder to resist than my plain old puppy eyes.

Once more Dr. Holland glanced at his watch. "Okay, Darshan, go ask your parents."

"Yes!" He tore across the field to his house, hoping to catch his parents before they left for work. In no time at all he returned with a broad grin. "They said yes, as long as I wear a life jacket." His father and mother waved to us from their porch.

So the OER agents, Dr. Holland, Darshan and I boarded the craft. There were no actual seats. Darshan and I perched along one side, and Dr. Holland faced us on the other. Julia sat in the back to operate the motor, and Eli took the front. At our feet was a variety of equipment we'd be using to conduct research.

In my excitement I bounced up and down as if I were sitting on a giant rubber ball, causing Darshan to spring up next to me. He grabbed onto the nylon rope fastened around the outer perimeter of the boat.

"We'll both fly off if you don't cut that out," he said. "And you really should buckle your life jacket." I snapped it shut across my chest and waist. It was an adult small size, but still way too big for me.

In spite of this perfect, sunny day, ours was the only craft on the lake due to the temporary restrictions. The lake was calm, and we glided smoothly across the surface. A few early morning joggers waved hello from the beach path.

Dr. Holland continued to watch the shore anxiously as we moved farther and farther from the dock. "I guarantee you," he said, "even though it's his own fault he missed the boat, somehow Dr. Mertz will find a reason to blame me. And if by some miracle we find fish, he'll never forgive me."

"Do you think we will? Find fish, that is."

"Alex, if there's a school of your fish somewhere in Glacial Lake, our goal is to locate them. Although our diver scouts found no evidence of any, this boat can cover a much larger area, and it's equipped with a sonar device that will sense any movement under the water. If one fish was washed down from the mountain, it's entirely possible that others might have been also."

I bounced again, feeling giggly. "They're down there, I just know it."

"Don't get too excited," Dr. Holland cautioned. "But even if nothing turns up, we'll still be doing other important research that could help us figure out where the fish came from."

The motor hummed as Julia zigzagged across the lake.

"Darshan, take a picture of me," I said, pulling a cell phone in a plastic bag from the pocket of my windbreaker. "Grandpa has got to see me here in a boat with all these marine life experts and fancy toys."

"I thought you broke your phone," he said. He sat at an angle, one hand clutching the safety rope around the boat.

"I did. Mom lent me her iPhone as long as I promised to be careful. Hence, the Ziploc bag!" I wiggled it in front of his face, and then took out the phone. "Plus, it has this heavy-duty, water-resistant case, so even if I splash water on it, it'll be okay."

"Why didn't you just bring your camera?" he asked.

I sighed, remembering the Nikon I had begged for and received on my last birthday. "I broke it on a fishing trip with

Grandpa. Slipped on gooey fish guts that some idiot left on the pier. I was just about to take a photo of Grandpa with his catch. You should've seen it—a huge salmon, this big!" I flung my arms wide, sending Mom's phone sailing into the lake.

Oops.

CHAPTER 18

"This piece of equipment is called a Side-Scan Sonar," Eli explained. "The device sends out pulses of sound. As those sound waves bounce off of objects—whether living things or the bottom of the lake—they reflect back to the boat and produce images of the shapes. It can be used for measuring depth, mapping the ocean floor, and tracking schools of fish."

We both leaned in for a closer inspection of the digital monitor.

"So it's like an underwater radar?" Darshan asked.

"Exactly."

"I don't get it," I said, feeling a bit frustrated. "How do bouncing sound waves tell us how deep the water is?"

Eli was as patient as my science teacher. "The computer in the machine measures the time it takes for the sound wave to reach the bottom of the lake and back. Then it converts the time to distance. It's like throwing a ball against a wall, catching it, and then figuring the distance the ball traveled."

"Can I work it?" said Darshan.

Uh! My shoulders slumped. I wanted to do it, but he asked first.

"Sure," Eli said. "You read out the numbers and I will record them in my notebook."

As Julia piloted the boat, cruising from shore to shore, Darshan's eyes remained glued to the monitor. "25 feet…45…65…75…55…40…25…," he called out. Eli recorded the measurements next to the exact coordinates determined by the GPS.

"You know," Dr. Holland said, bending over the side to let his hand dangle in the cool water, "some years back I took measurements of the lake with my students, but we didn't have such fancy equipment. We just used a long, weighted cord that had knots and tags indicating the depth."

"What did you come up with?" I asked.

"So far those prior measurements seem to match what we're recording now. We calculated the deepest part of the lake to be about 75 feet at the center. Of course we had only a row boat and couldn't cover as much area."

"Should we go out that way?" I suggested, indicating a little rocky island near a cliff. "I never see any boats or swimmers near there."

"Most boats would have trouble maneuvering around those rocks, so they stay clear of that area. But I think this little dinghy shouldn't have a problem if we go very slowly," Eli said.

Julia gave a thumbs-up and navigated around the rocks. Eli continued to jot the numbers as Darshan called them out. "45… 50…60…"

Suddenly Darshan yelled: "135 feet!"

Dr. Holland raised his eyebrows. "What? That can't be right. Check again."

Eli craned to get a good view of the monitor. He jiggled it and tapped the glass. He looked back up at Dr. Holland and nodded. "Seems to be working okay."

"The drop was sudden," said Julia. "We must be over a big hole of some sort." She shut off the motor and let the boat float quietly in the shadow of the cliff. All eyes lingered on the sonar readout.

"Okay, sailors, let's see what we have here," said Dr. Holland. He motioned to Julia. She started up the motor again.

For the next two hours we wove back and forth over what we determined to be a trench nearly a quarter mile long, about 30 feet at its widest, and at least 145 feet deep.

"What is it?" I asked.

"It's a fault, Alexis," said Dr. Holland.

I stiffened. "What's my fault? What did I do?"

"Ha, ha!" laughed Darshan. "I think he means a *volcanic* fault."

"I knew that," I muttered through gritted teeth.

"Of course you did," said Dr. Holland. "And this means we have yet more research to do. It's possible we have been wrong all along about the source of the high mineral concentrations in this lake. Rather than being caused by rain wash-out from the surrounding mountains, the minerals might originate directly from this crack."

"Maybe this is where my fish came from," I said. "There could be gobs of them down there."

Eli kept his eyes glued to the sonar monitor. "I doubt it, Alex. I haven't detected any movement."

"Eli, can we get a water sample from this spot?" asked Dr. Holland.

"Can I do it, please?" I begged. "Darshan got to record the sonar readings."

I stood up, but it was like standing in a party bouncy house and I toppled over. Darshan helped me up, and the boat rocked back and forth as we clumsily switched places. This put me closer to Eli so he could explain how to operate the equipment.

"This is a deep-water sampling device. As you can see, it has a weight clipped to the bottom, so it'll sink easily." He placed the vessel in my hands. Inside the clear outer chamber was a collection bottle with a stopper on the top.

85

"Notice down here," he said, turning the vessel over in my hands, "there is a thermometer that will record the temperature of the sample. And the attached cable is calibrated to show the depth as you lower the container. When it reaches the desired depth, pull this little lever and it will open the stopper. The bottle will fill with water. Release the lever and the stopper will close again. Go ahead, give it a try."

I played with the lever. Open, close, open, close. "That's easy."

"You got it," said Eli. "Then you reel it up like so. If we want samples from other areas, we remove the sample bottle from the apparatus, put in an empty one, then drop it down again."

I lowered the clear container, down, down, down into the depths. It seemed to take forever to drop 145 feet.

I was nervous about handling the expensive equipment, considering my history with cameras and phones. But my end of the line was anchored to the boat, so I couldn't accidentally drop it in. Once the container reached its destination depth, I squeezed the lever, and a few seconds later, released it.

"Okay, let's pull it up," said Eli.

With great care, I reeled it in. When it broke the surface, I reached over the boat to lift it from the water. "Ow!" I cried out. I dropped the container onto the floor of the boat. "This thing is boiling hot!"

CHAPTER 19

"No way," said Darshan. He touched it and quickly withdrew his hand. "She's right."

Each of the others touched the vessel. It was like a steamy little tea pot. Everyone stared mutely at the water container on the floor of the boat, as if it were a genie in a bottle. I bent forward to lift it by the cable, and held it in front of my nose to read the temperature. "It's almost 200 degrees!"

Dr. Holland took the device from me by its cable and examined it. He double-checked the numbers on the sonar monitor and scratched his head. Then his eyes danced with excitement. "My friends, it seems that we've stumbled upon the real secret of Glacial Lake. Hot gases and chemicals are bubbling up from a fault right beneath us!"

"Wait, what?" I asked. "You mean like an active volcano?"

"That's exactly what I mean. A geothermal spring, or a hot spring. Like the geysers in Yellowstone Park, but without the drama."

Darshan peered over the side of the boat. "Whoa! So cool!"

I agreed. "This is almost as cool as finding more fish. Not quite, but almost."

Dr. Holland chuckled. "I'm *not* looking forward to Mertz's reaction when realizes he wasn't here to claim this discovery." Without another word, he kicked off his sandals, peeled off his shirt and dove into the water. "Whoohoo! It's a virtual Jacuzzi in this spot," he shouted.

I gasped. "It's going to cook you!"

"Only if I dive down 145 feet. Don't worry, it's a bubbling brew on the bottom, but only lukewarm here at the surface."

We hooted as Dr. Holland treaded water, jibber-jabbering about percolating gases and simmering mineral particles. "…And this explains both Glacial Lake's relative warmth compared to surrounding mountain lakes, and its super-high mineral content, too."

A minute later, Eli and Darshan had removed their shirts and jumped in the water. Fully clothed, Julia and I followed.

From half a mile away we could see Dr. Mertz pacing at the dock. A few minutes later, the five of us waded to shore dragging the rubber boat over the rocks. Dr. Mertz waited with arms crossed, lips pressed tight, barrel chest heaving with every breath. That vein crawled down his forehead like an angry blue earthworm.

Dr. Holland reached into the boat and lifted the case containing the water samples. His eyes were fixed on Dr. Mertz. "Time to face the music," he mumbled.

"Go ahead, we'll take care of the boat," said Julia. She and Eli removed the motor and loaded the equipment into the truck. Holland strode toward Mertz.

"I've got to get home," Darshan said to me nervously.

"Oh, no you don't. We're not going to let Dr. Holland face Old Glory alone." I grabbed his hand and led him toward the two men.

"What's the idea of leaving me behind?" demanded Dr. Mertz. He spoke in a low, gravelly voice. "I've been waiting here since ten o'clock."

"The plan was to leave at nine, not ten," insisted Dr. Holland. "We waited till nine-thirty."

"Don't even try. This was intentional. You have been undermining me from the moment that darned kid found the fish."

"*That darned kid?*" I said a little too loudly, fists to my hips. "Hey, I'm standing right here, you know!"

"Alex, he doesn't mean it like that," said Dr. Holland. "He's just upset that—"

"Darned right I'm upset," Old Glory cut in. "Every step of the way I'm being shut out of the very research I am leading."

"With all due respect," said Dr. Holland, "the time was very clear in the email that came directly from the OER. I got the same email that you did. Go back and check it. Plus, I tried to call you several times until we simply had to take off, or else cancel. Please, check your messages."

Mertz's mustache wiggled as his mouth twitched. "Just give me those water samples. I'm taking them to the lab for analysis."

Behind us we heard a long *hisssss* and we all turned to watch the boat deflate into a blob of rubber. Dr. Holland's eyes were still on the boat when Mertz snatched the water samples and strode toward his car. Halfway there, he glanced back over his shoulder.

"By the way," he called out, "the fish is dead."

****

"It's gone, Grandpa," I wept. "Dead. Here one day, and poof! Gone the next. Far away from its home and family. Poor, poor fish." A little hiccup escaped my throat. "I didn't even get to say goodbye."

"I'm sorry, Minnow. I know it meant a lot to you. But don't you think you're being a tad melodramatic?"

"I am *not* being dramatic," I sobbed. "You don't understand, Grandpa. I discovered a brand new species of fish, and just days later, it's all over. How do you expect me to feel? I should have kept it in the bathtub and taken care of it myself, but I abandoned it to an institution and now it's dead and gone. An innocent life over, and I'm responsible."

Grandpa cleared his throat. "Hmm. You're right, Minnow. You're not being even the least bit dramatic."

"The truth is, everything I touch is doomed. Today I tossed Mom's phone to the bottom of the lake. Now I have to do the whole family's laundry all summer to earn enough to pay for it. Even Dad's boxer shorts. If you love me, Grandpa, you'll send Mom a new iPhone to relieve me of this torture."

"Not a chance," he said, but with kindness in his voice.

"It's okay, I forgive you." I wiped my nose on my shirt sleeve, and felt a little better having gotten it off my chest.

"There is one good thing, though. Today we found a volcanic fault and hot spring under Glacial Lake. Dad said to tell you that the warm mineral water is great for old, achy, weary bones. "

"Oh, did he now?" said Grandpa. "Then tell him *he* should go for a swim."

"Okay, I'll give him the message." I held back a laugh, since I wasn't quite ready to give up my bad mood.

"Well, goodnight, Grandpa."

"Goodnight, Minnow."

CHAPTER 20

The next day Darshan and I returned to Dr. Holland's office to discuss what would be happening next. His office door was closed, so we went to the room where my dearly departed fish had been. Some part of me hoped it was all a mistake—a bad dream—and my fish would still be there, climbing over stones and munching on brine shrimp. But the tank was empty. The water had already been drained.

Carla poked her head in the door. "Dr. Holland wants to see you two in his office." She motioned for us to follow. "Hey, sorry about the fish. We're all feeling pretty awful about it." She stroked my shoulder sympathetically as we walked.

"Me, too," I said. "I'm pretty bummed."

When we entered Dr. Holland's cluttered office, I found myself face to face with the dark-haired diver I had met at the lake a couple days before. He was even cuter dry. My heart raced. My palms started to sweat. His eyes were greener than I remembered. Like string beans. Or limes. Or mint ice cream…. Great, now I was hungry again.

"This is Gadi," said the professor. "He's a geology student from Israel, studying here at GLU. Besides a sharp brain, he has quite a few useful talents that we're utilizing."

"We've already had the pleasure of meeting. Hello, Alexis."

I loved his adorable accent, and the way he said my name. *Ah-lex-ees*."

He smiled broadly at me, flashing straight white teeth. Heat rose in my neck and face.

Thankfully the professor seemed not to notice and got on with the business. "Last night we reviewed what we know about the Walking Fish fossil, which unfortunately isn't much. The fossil was, in fact, found very near Glacial Lake, and the characteristics of Alex's fish point to it being a closely related species, if not the same one. We're now pretty certain the specimen Alex found could not have come from the lake, so we're expanding our search."

Gadi unrolled a large map of the area. He handed it to Dr. Holland who scanned the messy room for an open space to lay it out. His desk was littered with papers and folders. Files and books sat in piles on the floor around the desk and on the few chairs that were scattered around the office.

He moved to the wall, searching for a spot to pin the map up instead, but the walls were like a mural of diplomas, family photos, and charts. Even the window was plastered with Post-It notes. Finally, Dr. Holland dropped to his hands and knees, shoved away a mound of books and flattened out the map in the middle of the floor. We joined him on the threadbare carpet. Everyone's eyes were on the map, except for mine, which were locked on the superhero. *Scubaman.*

When I finally looked up, I realized that Darshan had been watching me watching Gadi.

"What?" I snapped. Darshan lowered his gaze back to the map on the floor.

Dr. Holland said, "We've highlighted the locations of several caves in the mountains surrounding Glacial Lake. "Here. Here. Here." With each "here," he poked at a spot on the map. Then he smacked Gadi on the back. "Gadi has been kind enough to recruit a number of volunteers to help us study a few of the caves. Not only is he a scientist and a scuba diver, he's also a member of the local spelunking club."

"The spelling club? How can they help?" I asked.

"Ezeh keta!" Gadi laughed. "It's *spelunking*. That's cave exploring."

For the second time in five minutes, I felt my face flush. Though I didn't understand the Hebrew, one thing was clear: I'd just made a fool of myself.

"Alexis, would you and Darshan like to join the study with the cave club?" asked Gadi. "Your friend Carla here is also a member. She'll be coming, too. In fact, she's the one who suggested that you join us."

In spite of my stupid question, he was inviting me along! It was a chance to redeem myself.

"Heck, yeah!" I said. "What do you say, Dar?"

Darshan didn't answer. Instead he asked, "What exactly will you be looking for in the caves?"

Dr. Holland used a yellow highlighter to mark the areas where the search would begin. "The first step will be to identify which caves contain bodies of water. Then, with permission from the appropriate state and county departments, as well as private land owners, we'll put nontoxic, biodegradable dyes in them. We might be able to determine which ones flow into Glacial Lake, or other nearby bodies of water, by the color of the water runoff."

Dr. Holland stood, rolled up the map, and handed it back to Gadi.

"What does Dr. Mertz have to say about all this?" asked Carla, who had found a seat on a corner of Dr. Holland's desk.

"He thinks it's a good plan. Of course, that's because I made him think it was *his* idea. He insists on supervising all aspects of the research. Maybe he hopes to find more of the Alex Fish in the caves."

Sure, I thought. *So he can change the name of my fish to the Mertz Fish.*

At lunchtime, Darshan and I sat in a courtyard outside the science building and opened the meal Mom had packed (quinoa black bean burgers and quinoa fig pudding. Seriously.) It was a warm, cloudless day, and we found a picnic table under a tree.

"Are you excited about going spelunking?" I asked. I bit into the veggie burger and had to admit it was really good.

"I'm not going. I'm busy that day," he said.

"You don't even know yet what day it'll be. What's the story? Hey…are you claustrophobic?"

"No," murmured Darshan.

"Then what?"

He threw up his arms. "Alex, you know very well my mother won't let me go. Ever since my father's accident, she treats me like I'm made of glass."

I narrowed my eyes accusingly. "You haven't even asked her. I know when you're lying. Tell me the truth."

Darshan drew in a slow breath. "Okay, it's the bats. They creep me out."

"No way. Come on, Dar, don't be such a wimp. Bats are cool. Besides, they eat bugs, not boys." I grinned and punched his arm. He couldn't be convinced.

After lunch, Darshan went in to help Carla in the lab. I decided to take a walk to Glacial Village Library a few blocks from the university. It was housed in an old colonial mansion with ivy climbing up the stone walls and lion statues guarding the front steps.

"Miss Tina?" I said, standing in front of the librarian's desk. The small, gray-haired woman was focused on taping a rip in a Dr. Seuss book.

"Miss Tina?" I repeated, louder this time.

"Oh!" The librarian looked up, startled, and studied me for a few moments. I waited in front of her desk until a look of recognition came over her face.

"Alexis! Hello, dear," Tina said, way too loudly. She clutched her cane and tottered around the desk to embrace me. "I thought you would have come to see me sooner. Of course, from what I understand, you've been much too busy for that, haven't you? It's so exciting to read about your discovery."

Nearby library patrons looked our way. Were they curious about the discovery, or just irritated by the volume of the Miss Tina's voice?

"It died," I said.

"Eh?"

"I said it died. The fish. Did you hear about that?"

"I did, dear." Tina took my hand in hers. "So sorry the little guy didn't make it."

"Thanks." My belly knotted again with sadness.

"What happens now?" asked Tina. "With the fish, I mean."

I explained that the department head, Dr. Mertz, would be examining the carcass. He would have it X-rayed, DNA tested, and preserved in the Environmental Sciences department. He would also lead the search for more fish. This would, of course, keep him front and center of any new discoveries.

"It's been pretty cool so far. I got to meet the governor, who happens to be really nice. Then I went on an inflatable boat and we found a hot spring under Glacial Lake. And next I'll be spelunk-ing!"

Tina tilted her head. "The Spelling King?" she asked. "You?"

I leaned closer. "No, no. I said I'm going *spelunking.*"

"Yes, indeed, you are spunky!" Tina bellowed.

A woman with her nose in a *Divorce for Dummies* book shot an annoyed glance. "Shhh!" she hissed.

That's a switch, I thought. *Hushing the librarian.* "Miss Tina, you aren't wearing your hearing aids, are you?"

Tina shuffled back around her desk. She reached inside her top drawer, pushed back her snowy hair, and popped a hearing aid into each ear. "Alrighty then, what did you say you're going to do?"

"I said I'm going spelunking. That's cave exploring, you know."

"Ah, let me guess—you want to check out some books on caves, right? Let's see what we have." Tina searched the computer catalog. Her fingers clickity-clacked briskly across the keys, in to-tal contrast to all her other snail-paced movements. While scan-ning the monitor for titles she said, "By the way, I came across an article in our archives you may find interesting. It's about a very peculiar fish. Some fishermen caught it deep in the ocean off the coast of Africa. Like yours, it turned out to be one that everyone thought was long ago extinct, with only fossils of it in museums. I knew you'd be coming in, so I saved it for you."

She slid the printed article across the desk to me. "Here, read it while I get those cave books for you." She rolled her chair from the desk, grabbed her cane, and hobbled to the stacks. This would take a while.

I made myself comfortable at a table and read the *New York Times* article about the "coelacanth," a hundred-pound, hard-scaled, flesh-eating fish. It was unbelievably ugly. *Luckily it only has to be attractive to another fish,* I thought. I wondered how they caught it more than two hundred feet beneath the ocean.

Tina came back balancing a load of books in one arm, and clutching a cane in her free hand.

"Oh, sorry, Miss Tina! I should have been helping you with that." I jumped from my chair and took the books from her.

"Nonsense," she said. "I do this all day long. It's great exercise. How do you think I maintain these huge muscles?" She flexed her arm. It had an impressive little hump, in spite of the curtain of skin jiggling beneath her arm. "Now tell me about the Walking Fish."

I plucked a scrap of paper from the waste basket and drew a picture of my fish. "It was about ten inches long and sort of a light pink. And it used long feelers to explore, like this." I wiggled the fingers of one hand in front of my chin.

Two small kids laughed at me from a nearby table. Encouraged by my audience, I went on. "And it had a blowhole, kind of like a whale or a dolphin." I opened and closed my fist atop my head to imitate it. "And its pelvic fins—the ones on the bottom—were like strange little feet that it used to climb over rocks, like this." I dropped to my belly and crawled over a beanbag chair to demonstrate, all the while wiggling my "feelers" in front of me. The giggling children fell to the floor and crawled along behind me.

"Did I mention that my fish had no eyes? Yep, blind as a bat." I closed my eyes and crawled through the picture book aisle, followed by a growing line of children with wiggling fingers and eyes squeezed shut.

"As a matter of fact, bats aren't blind," Tina said.

"They're not?"

"No. Says so right here." She stuck a cave book under my nose. I read the caption beneath a photo of a bat.

"Well, lookie there, you're right!" I shrugged. "Never mind then. My fish was blind as a…as a…as a fish with no eyes." The children and I continued our Walking Fish crawl through the stacks until I bumped my cheek on a shelf of Beverly Cleary chapter books. "Well, the fish did it much better, but it had a lot more practice."

Tina chuckled. "All right, off the floor, all of you. This is a library, not a playground."

I grabbed the cave books that she had selected for me and found a cozy nook to read in. The kids' section, with its bright colors and soft-padded rocking chairs, was my favorite area. During my first summer at Glacial Lake, when I was really young, I had announced to Tina my plan to read all of the books in the library in alphabetical order. When I discovered that the first books were on "abstract architecture" and "aeronautical engineering," I revised the plan to include only the books in the youth department. Ultimately, I settled on a reading list that Tina put together for me.

"I'm guessing you'll be too busy to read much this summer," said Tina. She had come over to check on my progress. Though most of the books in my pile were nonfiction, she found me engrossed in an adventure novel about a teenager who got lost in a cave after going in alone. The girl barely made it out alive.

"Consider that one a cautionary tale," said Tina with a wink.

At four o'clock I went to the counter to check out several books.

Tina eyed the titles. "What about the adventure novel? Don't you want to take it home, too?" she asked.

I handed her my library card. "Already finished it," I said. "Not a bad story."

Though not nearly as exciting as my own cave adventure would prove to be.

CHAPTER 21

The open Jeep snaked up the road toward Camel Hump Mountain, the tallest mountain bordering Glacial Lake. My hair whipped behind me as I lifted my face into the wind. When the road began to twist and turn, so did my stomach. I moaned.

"You are an interesting shade of green," Gadi said from the driver seat. "Are you carsick?"

I nodded almost imperceptibly, as if simply moving my head would cause me to throw up. "Maybe you should pull over. I think I might puke."

Dr. Mertz sat in the front passenger seat, and through the rearview mirror I saw him roll his eyes like a teenage girl. But he said nothing as Gadi eased onto the shoulder of the road.

"Here, have a drink." Gadi twisted open the cap of a water bottle and handed it to me. "Aren't you used to traveling these roads? You've been coming here for years."

I took a small sip, making sure it stayed down before taking another. "I *am* used to the roads. I'm just not used to your driving."

Gadi laughed. "Okay, I'll slow it down a bit. If you do lose your lunch, aim outside the Jeep."

After a few minutes, I felt ready to continue and Gadi pulled back onto the road. I caught an occasional glimpse of the southern part of the lake, until the road curved a final time and the lake was completely hidden by the mountain.

At some point Gadi turned off the main highway and we continued along a dirt path.

"Those signs say 'No Trespassing,'" I said. "Are we allowed to be here?"

"The cave is on private land, but the owner has given us permission to be here."

The Jeep plowed over gravel and ruts along the final stretch to our destination. We came to a stop next to a mud-spattered pickup truck.

"*Yallah*, everybody out. We hike the rest of the way," Gadi announced. He and I grabbed our backpacks. Old Glory, on the other hand, stepped from the car and made no move to help with the gear. He hadn't said a word the entire drive.

"Grab that, will you, kid?" Mertz barked, pointing to a small duffle on the floor of the front seat. I retrieved it and held it out to him. Rather than taking it, he abruptly spun on his heels and headed toward another car in the parking area, leaving me to carry his bag along with my own.

A tall, skinny kid with wild blond hair was waiting for us in the parking area. He appeared to be barely older than I was.

"Where've you all been?" the kid asked Gadi. His annoyed tone surprised me. "You were supposed to be here at eleven."

"It's only 11:05, Simon," said Gadi.

"Exactly. You're throwing us off schedule."

Gadi seemed undisturbed by Simon's rudeness and ignored the comment. "*Nu?* Where's Carla?" he asked.

"Waiting at the cave with the equipment. I came down to wait for you, in case you forgot the way."

"I know the way, but thanks," said Gadi. He turned to us. "Dr. Mertz, Alexis—this is Simon, another geology student at the university, and a fellow member of the Glacial Lake Spelunking Club. He's been involved in mapping this cave, so he knows it better than anyone."

Mertz nodded. His eyes focused somewhere over Simon's shoulder.

"Hi," I said.

Simon did not return my greeting. Instead he said flatly, "Our mission today is to collect rocks, fungi and other specimens from a small lake inside the cave." He looked from me to Dr. Mertz as he cleaned an ear with his little finger.

When he said nothing more, I said, "Dr. Holland mentioned that this caving expedition could help us learn about the fish's environment, and maybe its food sources. Does this mean we might find some fish as well?"

Simon shook his head so vigorously that you'd think he was shaking a fly off his nose. "That's not our mission. You can't expect to wander into a cave and stumble upon something like that. We have to be very systematic on a mission like this."

My face fell with disappointment. I had hoped we'd find a whole school of Walking Fish. Simon pivoted and began trekking up the mountain. He apparently expected everyone to follow him without being told. And we did.

I grumbled to Gadi, "What's this 'mission' business? He must think this is the FBI."

"You're upset we won't be searching for fish, aren't you?" Gadi asked.

I shrugged. "Nah, I guess not. Or at least, I shouldn't be. I mean, a few days ago I'd never heard of a spelunker and today I am one. That's pretty cool."

Two other teams were investigating other caverns in the surrounding mountains. If none of this led to the Walking Fish, at least I had been assigned to Gadi's group. I was surprised Dr. Mertz let me go at all, but so far he was keeping his promise. Probably just so he'd have someone to carry his stuff.

I scurried a few steps to catch up to Gadi and Simon. My short little legs had to take nearly two steps for every one of theirs.

"*Nu?* Why do you have that?" Gadi asked, noticing that I was carrying Mertz's bag. He slipped it from my shoulder and slung it around his own. Then he picked up a narrow branch and broke a bit off one end, making it the perfect size for a walking stick. "Here you go."

"Thanks," I said, taking it from him. Behind us Dr. Mertz huffed and puffed his way up the mountain. For someone so out of shape, he seemed pretty determined to keep up. I walked faster.

"Hey, Simon, what are the other two teams doing?" I asked.

"Their mission is to seek out hidden water sources in some of the less explored caves surrounding Glacial Lake. We haven't finished mapping this cave, but there is a lake inside. I've never seen fish in it, though. If anyone finds cave fish today, it'll probably be one of the other groups." Then he grumbled, "Those other teams get to do the *really* fun stuff, like rappelling down tunnels with ropes."

"If you think it's so much fun, why aren't you with them instead?" I asked.

"My mother won't let me."

I squinted at him, confused. "But you're in college."

"Yes," he answered. I waited for him to elaborate. He didn't. I glanced at Gadi, who only shrugged.

"Okaaaay," I said, feeling a little impatient. "How old are you, anyway?"

"Fifteen," said Simon.

"*What?*"

"Fifteen," he repeated.

"I heard you the first time. But you said you're in college."

"Yes," he said, still offering no explanation.

Gadi laughed, seeing my bewilderment. "Our Simon is unique. Hey, why don't you guys take a break so Dr. Mertz can catch up. I'll go ahead to get things ready."

I would have been happy to leave Old Glory behind, but in truth, I could use a little rest myself. Simon leaned against a tree while I plopped down on a log. The professor grunted and wheezed as he made his way toward us.

"One thing's for sure," I said to Simon, "he's not a quitter."

"Even if he weren't obese, he'd be having trouble keeping up at his age," said Simon matter-of-factly twisting his little finger in his ear again. "Studies show that men hit their peak muscle mass in their thirties, and then lose about five pounds of muscle per decade after age forty. The lower muscle mass affects the body's ability to burn calories and usually results in an increase in fat, which brings with it problems such as diabetes, joint pain, and heart disease."

I could only stare at this strange boy, who shifted awkwardly from foot to foot before adding, "I'm just saying, that's why Dr. Mertz is lagging behind."

I smiled and nodded.

When Mertz reached us, we waited till he caught his breath before continuing our ascent. This time I slowed my pace so he could keep up.

"Samuel, how far to the cave?" asked Mertz. Sweat dripped into his eyes and down his neck. He swiped at it with the back of his hand.

Simon eyed him blankly. "It's Simon, not Samuel."

"Whatever," Mertz raised his hand dismissively. "Just tell me, how far do we have to go?"

"For me, it's a total of 2,150 steps from the parking spot to the mouth of the cave. But it varies from person to person. For instance, Alex has a shorter stride. I'd estimate perhaps 2,900 of her steps, give or take—"

Mertz clenched his fists. "For goodness sake, boy, I meant how much *farther*?"

Simon raised an eyebrow. "Well, if you had let me finish, I was going to say we're about 95 percent there."

Soon afterward we approached a huge boulder with a yellow bat painted on it. Just around the rock we met up with Gadi. He was chatting with Carla, the final member of the team.

Carla hugged me as if we were old friends. "Hey, girl. I'm glad you could make it!" she said.

Dr. Mertz introduced himself to Carla without extending his hand.

"Hello, I'm *Dr.* Mertz," he said stiffly. He stressed the word "doctor."

"I guess you don't remember, but I've taken some of your classes," said Carla.

"Of course."

"You and Alex are going to love Teles Cave," she said, bending down to tighten the laces of her boots.

"Why is it called Teles Cave?" I asked.

"It's named after our very own Simon Teles," said Gadi, slapping Simon on the back. Simon stumbled forward a bit. "Our boy here discovered it."

"No way," I said. "Simon, *you* found this cave? How?"

He shrugged. "Rock collecting. Fossil hunting. I've spent a lot of time alone up in these mountains."

"That is *so* cool to have a cave named after you," I said.

He raised a shoulder, as if it were no big deal, and reached into an army-style duffle bag. He passed out helmets with attached headlamps as he rattled off a supply checklist.

"Everyone should have a minimum of two flashlights, spare flashlight bulbs, and extra batteries for this mission. Please check now."

Gadi had provided me with a supply list the day before, so I had come prepared. Simon instructed everyone to switch on each flashlight to make sure they were all in working order. Next he checked the expiration dates on the batteries, even though they were in brand new, unopened packages. Dr. Mertz grumbled something I couldn't hear. Probably the same thing I was thinking.

"I expect you all brought drinking water," Simon continued. "One bottle each should do it—we'll only be in there a couple of hours. You should also have thick gloves, preferably waterproof. If you didn't bring any, you're out of luck since I don't have any spares. And you better have a sweatshirt or jacket lest you succumb to hypothermia. Symptoms of hypothermia include shivering, mental confusion—"

"Simon!" Dr. Mertz snapped. "We've all brought the proper outfits. You can skip the medical lesson."

"Fine," Simon said, without so much as glancing at Dr. Mertz. He unfolded a hand-drawn map and held it up against a tree trunk. "This first area is a passage that extends into the mountain for about fifty yards. It drops in elevation as it winds around a bit before opening into a huge cavern."

He ran his finger along the outline of the underground lake, which filled two-thirds of the cave room. "At this end here, the cavern wall drops down to, or below, the surface of Teles Lake."

"Teles Lake?" I exclaimed. "You even have a lake named after you? That's awesome! How about bats? Are there Teles bats in Teles Cave?"

Simon rubbed his forehead. "I have not seen a bat colony in this cave, but that doesn't mean there aren't any. Regardless, they wouldn't be named after me. May I continue now?" He obviously didn't like being interrupted.

I nodded sheepishly.

Simon went on. "We haven't been able to explore past that wall, so we don't know how far the lake extends. Our research will take place along the bank, and over a few ledges extending from the walls."

He folded the map and stuck it in his back pocket. "If anyone has to pee, find a tree now since you can't go again till we're out of the cave. Do not—I repeat, do not—leave toilet paper in the woods. It takes two to four months for toilet paper to decompose. That's nothing compared to your plastic water bottle, which would take 450 to 1000 years to biodegrade, so I hope I don't need to remind you not to leave it behind either."

"Great, Simon, I think we've got it," said Gadi. "Helmets on, everyone. You can get pretty banged up in there." He set his own helmet on his head, clipped the chin strap, and flipped the switch of the headlamp. The rest of us did the same. "Wear your gloves. It can get muddy."

I was sweating from the summer heat, but when everyone else layered up with sweatshirts and jackets, I did as well.

Simon led us into the mouth of the cave. The entrance was hidden among the roots and rocks around it. Less than three feet in diameter, it was small enough that a hiker could easily walk right by and not notice it. Gadi went second, followed by me, Mertz and Carla. We entered by sitting on the ground and scooting in feet first. Once inside the first small room, I was able to stand.

"I call this part 'the foyer,'" said Simon.

I drew in a deep breath. The cave had a dank though not unpleasant smell, like wet earth after a rain. The cold air chilled my throat and nostrils. I was glad for the extra layers.

Simon advanced through the next passage to make room for Mertz and Carla. If this was the foyer, I guess the next section was a hallway. For the first several yards, light still filtered in from outside. Then the passage twisted and turned, and only the light from our headlamps illuminated the path. The walls were wet, as if they were sweating, and water trickled from cracks in the ceiling.

"Watch your heads," said Simon. "The ceiling drops low up ahead."

Dr. Mertz grunted as he stooped. I was the only one short enough to pass though without having to duck. I stumbled once or twice on the slippery damp ground, but caught myself before I fell.

I peered into a passage off to the right. "Where does this go?"

"No telling," said Simon. "There are a lot of channels that lead from the main one. Some are dead ends, but many intersect with other tunnels. We haven't surveyed them all yet."

Curious, I stepped in deeper to explore the passage. Gadi grabbed the hood of my jacket and pulled me back.

"Never veer off by yourself," he warned. "It's like a maze. You can easily get lost. It's very dangerous." I felt angry at myself for getting scolded a mere five minutes into the trip.

"Hey, cave spider to my left," said Carla. She aimed a beam to illuminate the creature. Like Simon, it had a thin body on long spindly legs. *The Teles spider*, I thought, smiling to myself. Mertz backed away nervously. He wouldn't even look at it.

"Oh, wow, check out the size of that thing," I said, showing off how much braver I was than Old Glory. I measured the creature against my hand. It was nearly the size of my palm. I wiggled my fingers trying to make it move, but it didn't budge from its spot on the cold wall. "Wish I had a camera."

"Here, use my cell phone," said Carla. "I'll send the pictures to you later." I snapped several shots of the critter and managed to return the phone safely.

We pushed deeper into the cave. The corridor became narrower. "I hear water," I said. It sounded distant and hollow, like an echo.

"You're hearing a waterfall that empties into the lake," said Carla. "We're close now. It's just a bit past that gap."

The passageway tapered until it was barely more than a crack. Simon pushed his pack through and dropped it to the other side. He had to duck to avoid hitting his head, but otherwise stepped through easily.

Gadi was next. He passed his bag to Simon and turned sideways in order for his broad shoulders to clear the slim opening. He motioned for me to go through next. "Hand me your backpack. On the other hand, you're such a twig that you can probably slip through with it on."

"Ahem! The word is 'petite,'" I corrected. But Gadi was right. By pressing my elbows together I stepped straight through the crevice with the pack still on my back.

Mertz was another story. When he reached the crevice, he couldn't squeeze through straight or sideways.

"Try taking off your jacket," suggested Carla. Mertz peeled it off and dropped it to the ground. He stuck an arm and a leg through the gap. Gadi grabbed his arm and pulled, while Carla pushed the professor from the other side.

"Take a deep breath, then force out all the air like you're deflating a balloon," I suggested. Defying the chill of the cave, beads of sweat appeared on Old Glory's temples.

It was no use.

"Sorry, you'll have to go back," said Simon. Carla will lead you out."

If his humiliation weren't bad enough, being bossed around by a fifteen-year-old was more than Mertz could bear. He exploded with anger.

"Go back? I will do no such thing. You said the lake is just a short distance past this wall, so I will wait right here. Every few minutes, one of you can report to me on the progress."

"No can do," said Simon. "You'll get too cold standing there for an hour. Even with the extra fatty insulation, at this temperature, hypothermia can set in within—"

"Save it, you little know-it-all," snapped Mertz. "Carla, let's go."

We listened to him mutter and curse until he was out of earshot. I burst out laughing.

"Be nice," said Gadi, though even in the dim light I thought I saw a smirk on his face.

"Okay, let's continue on," said Simon. "This fiasco has cost us four minutes and twenty seconds."

We continued through one last turn before reaching the final destination. Gadi had stopped ahead of me and blocked my view.

"*Ezeh yofi!*" he exclaimed.

"What? What is it?" I asked, wishing he'd stick with English.

"You're going to love this, it's so beautiful. And smile— you're on camera." He pressed a button to activate a tiny, helmet-mounted video camera before moving aside to let me through. I shined my light around the cavern.

What I saw took my breath away.

CHAPTER 22

The passage opened into a gigantic room. I figured my whole school, parking lot and all, could fit into it. Throughout the room, glistening stalactites hung from the ceiling like stone icicles. Some narrowed elegantly to rounded tips as they reached for the cave floor. Others were short and stubby. Drops of water clung to the ends, occasionally losing their grip and falling to the floor. *Plop...plop.*

Rising from the ground were stalagmites—rocky spears that were mirror images of the hanging formations. In some places, the pairs met to form glossy, sweating columns.

"Oh, wow," I said in a breathy whisper. I had seen pictures of cave decorations like these in the books that Tina had selected for me. Standing amidst them was more hauntingly beautiful than any photograph. It was surreal.

"I read about those," I said. "They're formed by minerals in the water—calcite or something, right?—that drip from cracks in the cave ceiling."

"Hey, smart girl," said Gadi. I was pleased that, for once, I'd managed to impress him rather than embarrass myself. I reached out to stroke one of the slender stalactites.

"No, don't touch!" said Gadi, snatching my hand away from the formation. "It takes about two hundred years for it to grow a single inch, and just a moment to be destroyed by human carelessness."

"Sorry," I muttered. So much for impressing Gadi. I was grateful for the darkness so that he couldn't see me blush.

Simon chimed in. "Besides keeping your hands to yourself, you also need to watch your step. If you fall and injure yourself, a cave rescue mission would be very difficult, and—"

"I'll be careful," I blurted. He was seriously starting to annoy me.

We made our way across the room until we reached what we had come for. The water shimmered in the glow of our lights, and all was silent except for the beautifully eerie splash and echo of water crashing over rocks.

Gadi directed a flashlight around the lake as he walked along the bank. At the far end, the cavern wall dropped all the way to the lake, just as Simon had described. There was no telling how far beyond the wall the lake extended. A few yards? A mile? Perhaps it even flowed into an underground river that emptied into Glacial Lake.

"See how high the water rose in here during the spring floods?" asked Simon, pointing up to a watermark on the wall. "I've been in this cave several times over the past three years, and the water level is still higher than I've ever seen it."

"Do you think that lakes in other caves around here rose as high as this one?" I asked.

"Absolutely."

Gadi added, "Dr. Holland is convinced that, in whatever cave these fish might reside, there's a fracture that extends all the way through the mountain to Glacial Lake." He shined the light up to the watermark. "Imagine if there were such a crack way up there, well above the usual water level inside the cave. Only when the water rose high enough to reach that crack, could the fish be washed through it and down to Glacial Lake."

I had a picture in my mind of my frightened fish being swept from its dark, quiet home, its poor body banged around as it was washed through rocky crevices. In my mind's eye I saw it plummet down the mountain into the lake, where it finally ended up trapped in an ever-shrinking pond. If it hadn't been sightless already, the bright sunlight would probably have made it go blind.

"There's no telling how many other fish could have been carried down along with the one you found," said Gadi, "if that is, in fact, what happened."

Simon cleared his throat. He had been getting antsy during the discussion, clicking his flashlight on and off. "Excuse me. We have a mission to complete."

We set to work collecting samples in plastic containers. The "mission" included using the tools in our bags to gather rocks, sediment, soil, and water samples.

Gadi assembled a net, attaching a short handle with a few twisting motions. He pulled on one end, and the telescoping handle expanded to four times its original length.

"The purpose of collecting sediment from the lake floor is to search for evidence of living organisms," he explained, scraping the net along the bottom of the lake. "If there are fish in here, or ever were, we might find small bones or fossils. But don't get your hopes up. It's unlikely."

Simon gave me a thermometer and instructed me to check the water temperature. As I knelt at the edge, I scanned the crystal clear water for signs of fish, just in case. *They said there are no fish in here, but they also said there weren't any in Glacial Lake,* I thought.

Gadi dumped a pile of sediment on the bank of the lake. Simon, on his knees, sifted through the muck. Over the next half hour Simon and Gadi plucked out a few tiny white shrimp. Determined to find something useful in the water also, I stepped cautiously onto a large rock to get a better view beneath the surface. Suddenly from my perch I heard a plop, and saw a ripple in the water.

"Simon! Gadi! Something jumped!" In my excitement, one foot slipped off the rock and sank into the lake up to my knee. I let out a yelp.

"Are you okay?" asked Gadi. "*Oy*, that's got to be cold."

I hopped to dry ground and shook the water from my foot. "Yes, it's really, really cold. But I *did* see something, right there."

All eyes were fixed on the spot where I pointed.

Plop.

Simon and Gadi saw it this time, in exactly the same place.

Plop.

There it was again. And again.

Gadi laughed. "It's water dripping from the ceiling. Sorry to disappoint you, Alex. And hardly worth the next hour in a wet boot."

With Gadi facing in my direction, I knew the stupid video camera attached to his helmet was recording every second of my humiliation. I could only hope it wouldn't end up on YouTube for all my friends to see. As hard as I fought the tears, a fat drop slipped down my cheek as I yanked off my boot to squeeze out my sock.

I was grateful when Simon's obsession with time diverted Gadi's attention from me. "We've been in here for fifty-two minutes. That's seven minutes behind schedule. Now we'll need to hurry in order to be out on time."

We gathered our gear and double-checked that no supplies were being left behind. Simon led the trek back to the cave entrance. The return trip seemed more like a mile because of my cold, wet foot. I dared not mention it again, however, for fear of a lecture from Simon on frostbite or foot fungus.

About thirty yards before reaching the exit, I felt something climbing up my pants. I stomped my leg violently, but whatever it was kept crawling toward my knee.

"Something's crawling…there's something inside…uh! It's in my pants!" I stammered, trying to hide the terror in my voice.

"Smack it," suggested Simon.

"Gross, no! It'll squish all over me. Or bite me." I wiggled. I shook. I kicked. "Ooh, I can't get it off!"

"Then remove your pants and brush it off," said Simon. He sounded annoyed, judgmental even, as if I were making a big deal about nothing.

"Take off my pants? Are you kidding?" I yelled. But that's what I did. I dropped my backpack and ducked into a narrow passage off to the side that dead-ended a few feet in. Frantically, I threw off my gloves, unzipped my jeans, and yanked my pants down to my knees. The spider jumped off my thigh and scampered across the ground, hiding beneath a rock.

"Ech." I shuddered and tugged my jeans back up over my hips. My right glove lay next to me, but in my panic I had thrown the left glove way ahead. When I squeezed to the end of the passage to retrieve it, I discovered a hole close to the ground that had not been noticeable from a standing position. Through the hole I heard a muffled splashing sound, similar to the waterfall at Teles Lake.

Simon called out. "Alex, now we're eleven minutes behind schedule." There was pressure in his voice, and I wondered what the big hurry was. *Maybe he needs to use the men's tree,* I thought. He should have followed his own advice and done his business before we entered the cave.

I backed out of the corridor and caught up with them, taking my place between Simon and Gadi. "I think there's something back there," I said.

"Probably," said Simon. He hurried ahead without asking about it. Maybe Gadi would be more interested, so I turned to him behind me. "I'm pretty sure I heard water. Shouldn't we check it out?"

"There's water all over this cave, Alexis, but we got what we came for and now we need to get the samples to the lab."

"Fine," I muttered. "Mission accomplished, right?" I dropped the subject, but made a point of counting the number of steps it took from that spot to reach the mouth of the cave.

The bright midday sun felt warm and pleasant after the cold, damp cavern. Carla sat on the ground with her back against a tree, playing a game on her cell phone. Dr. Mertz smoked a cigarette on a boulder in the shade. I wondered if there was any bad habit he didn't have.

Carla had left a cooler of sandwiches and chips outside the cave. It was surprising how much spelunking makes you work up an appetite. I chose a plain old PBJ, something I missed since Mom had abandoned the simple pleasures for gourmet cuisine. I longed to take off my wet boot, but my clean pair of shoes was down at the car, and besides, I hadn't brought extra socks.

After the snack break, our team filled the empty cooler with plastic jars containing water and sediment samples, plus the little shrimp collected from the muck. Gadi and Carla took turns carting the cooler. The rest of the equipment, plus a few rocks that may have contained small fossils, was distributed among our various backpacks.

Only Dr. Mertz didn't volunteer to carry anything. Maybe he felt he shouldn't have to since he didn't get to do the collecting.

On the way down the trail he said, "Hold this a minute while I tie my shoe, will you?" and shoved his backpack at me. Naturally, he didn't take it back, and I ended up carrying it along with my own.

The sun was now high in the sky. It was much hotter and our backpacks heavier, yet the trek downhill was quicker than it had been going up. With no extra space in our packs, we tied our jackets and sweatshirts around our waists. Only Simon kept his layers on, seemingly unbothered by the heat.

"Boots in here," ordered Gadi once we reached the car. He held open a large garbage bag for me and Dr. Mertz. "The mud stays *outside* my Jeep." We removed our grimy boots and changed into the sneakers we'd left in the car. Simon and Carla had come together, and changed their shoes and outerwear by Carla's car.

"Dr. Mertz, what kinds of tests will be done on the samples?" I asked on the drive back. "And when will all the tests be completed?"

"Lots of tests. It could take a while," he said.

Why did he have to be so vague? It was like he was intentionally keeping me in the dark. I decided to wait and ask Dr. Holland.

One thing was really gnawing at me though. "Gadi, I'm sure there was more water beyond that passage where I pulled down my…I mean, where I shooed the spider from my leg. Can we go back again later and check it out?"

Dr. Mertz spun around in his seat and narrowed his eyes. "You saw another body of water? Where?" He wouldn't answer my questions, yet he expected me to answer his. It figured.

"I didn't see it, but I heard it," I said. "Not far from the entrance, through a narrow side passage. I heard a waterfall or something, but didn't get a chance to look. Maybe we should return to investigate it."

Mertz settled back in his seat and shook his head. "That won't be necessary."

I closed my eyes. The wind blew the sweat from my face as I fantasized about bopping Old Glory on the head with my flashlight. I'd never do it though. It wasn't worth the risk of breaking my flashlight.

CHAPTER 23

"So it was super fun and all, Grandpa. I just wish we could have explored that mysterious passage. I know I heard water back there, but no one would listen to me. Nobody *ever* listens to me."

Pause.

"Grandpa?"

"Oh, sorry, were you saying something?"

"Grrr. Very funny. Goodnight, Grandpa."

"Goodnight, Minnow. By the way, I always listen to your every word."

****

I was wide awake before the break of dawn, and far too excited to stay in bed any longer. It was still dark when I slipped into my clothes and tiptoed onto the back porch. Soon the distant mountains were edged in pink and orange. When the sun topped the mountains to the east, I decided to go for a walk.

My daily pond inspections were, by now, more out of habit than any belief that I might discover something other than a wandering turtle or common frog. The smaller of the two ponds had become barely more than a big muddy puddle. But the larger pond—the one where I found my fish—continued to evaporate at a much slower rate. No one else seemed to have noticed.

I kicked off my shoes, rolled my pant legs up above my knees, and stepped into the cold water. By now I was familiar with every stone and dip. I scanned beneath the glistening water. Except for water bugs gliding across the surface, all was still.

Emerging from the pond with sandals in hand, I made my way toward the lake and waded in. The water was cold, though not as uncomfortable as the chill of the pond.

When my stomach began to rumble, I headed back to the cabin. The yellow-orange sun rose high, looking like James's Giant Peach floating in the cloudless sky. As I climbed the steps, the screen door opened and my mother stepped onto the porch. We sat together on the swing, watching the mountain cast shadows on the lake.

"When will they get here?" I asked, breaking the silence.

"They'll get here when they get here."

"Perfect day for a helicopter ride, don't you think?"

"Absolutely," said Mom. "It's also a perfect day for a three-cheese artichoke and mushroom omelet. How about if we whip some up together?"

"Sure." We went inside.

I grabbed a carton of eggs from the fridge and knocked them one by one against the edge of a bowl. *Crack, plop. Crack, plop.*

"One-handed egg cracking, Mom," I said. "Watch and learn."

Crack. The last egg shell crumbled into the bowl. I picked out bits of shell and whipped the goo.

Whop, whop, whop...

When the eggs were fluffy I stopped mixing, but the whipping sound continued. In fact, it got louder. *WHOP, WHOP, WHOP.*

"They're here!" I abandoned the bowl and dashed out to meet the helicopter on the large, flat plot of land between our cabin and the lake. There were only a few trees around the perimeter of the yard, and Dad and I had dragged our lawn furniture out of the way the night before. It was an ideal landing pad, and secluded enough to avoid curious spectators.

The aircraft, with the letters OER painted on its side, touched down close to the lake.

I made my way toward the aircraft, my hair blowing every which way in the wind created by the whirring blades. When the *whop, whop, whop* finally came to a stop, I heard the pilot radio, "Egg Beater One has landed." I imagined flipping those huge helicopter blades upside down into a giant bowl of gooey raw eggs.

Dr. Holland had been next door chatting with Darshan and his parents. Now he and Darshan headed toward our yard.

"Don't you dare get in that thing!" Darshan's mom yelled after him. "Remember, you promised!"

He had argued with her for days. "But Amma, they really are safe. You would have let me go before Appa's accident. Now you don't let me do anything fun."

Even my parents had tried to convince her, but she wouldn't give in. The invitation had been extended to both of us, but no matter how much he pleaded, she would not consent for him to fly in the helicopter.

"It's a wonder those contraptions stay up at all," she said. "It doesn't even have wings." She agreed that he could look inside and even sit in the pilot's seat if they let him, as long as he kept "far away from those decapitating blades" when it lifted off.

The pilot opened his door and Darshan was instantly at his side, asking questions about the controls. The OER agent in the front passenger seat stepped down from the copter, and introduced himself as Maurice Creston. He was about to brief us on the day's plan when a local reporter and cameraman appeared out of nowhere. The reporter's blond hair, dyed a few shades too light, clashed with her brown eyebrows. She wore contact lenses that turned her eyes an unreal shade of violet-blue. She looked like a Barbie doll, down to her freakishly small waist and feet.

The woman planted herself in the middle of the action and spoke into the camera. "Hello, I'm Leah Burgas, reporting from the shore of Glacial Lake. I'm here with a research team involved in locating the source of the so-called Walking Fish, discovered only days ago at this exact spot."

She abruptly held her microphone in front of Maurice Creston's face. "Can you tell us what will be happening here today?"

Maurice looked at her to answer, but the reporter indicated, with a slight tilt of her head, that he should face the camera instead.

He shifted and cleared his throat. "Well, Leah, during the past few days, geologists and spelunkers have explored a number of the caves in the mountains surrounding Glacial Lake. They found streams and ponds in a few of those caves. This morning, researchers have gone back to those underground waters to dump in barrels of dye—a different color for each area."

"How will it affect the area's water supply?" Leah asked. Again Maurice turned to her. This time Leah reminded him with subtle pointing of her microphone to look at the camera instead of her.

"This is a biodegradable vegetable dye. It's nontoxic and harmless, and will disappear within several hours, or a day, max. Any discoloration in a stream, water supply, or well is not a reason for concern. The water is safe to drink."

Leah nodded approvingly and narrated into the rolling camera. "While officials will be gathering most of the information from the air, residents and visitors are asked to call the special hotline you see on your screen to report any discoloration noted

123

in streams and wells. With your help, scientists can determine the path of any water that originates in the caves. We hope this will lead researchers to the home of Glacial Lake's very special Walking Fish."

She made a slash sign across her neck, signaling the cameraman to stop recording. "Good luck, and be careful up there," she said to the agent, and she disappeared with her news crew.

A few minutes later, I took a seat behind Maurice. "Here, put these on," he said, handing me a set of noise-reducing earmuffs.

Dr. Holland remained on the lawn. "Aren't you coming?" I asked.

"Wish I could," he said. "Unfortunately, too much loud rock music in my youth damaged my ears drums. I'm afraid the noise and altitude will only make it worse. I'm better off waiting for you here on the ground."

"Why isn't Dr. Mertz coming, then? There's room for one more." As nasty as Old Glory could be, he had kept his word and arranged for me to go on the helicopter ride, and for that I was grateful.

"He had an important meeting today, but asked me to wish you a good trip," said Dr. Holland. He waved and strolled away with Darshan to join our parents.

Whop, whop, whop. The blades began to spin again. My heart pounded and my stomach flip-flopped as the helicopter quivered, hovered briefly, and rose into the air.

"I can't believe Dr. Mertz would miss this for some dumb meeting," I yelled to Maurice over the noise. "Couldn't he reschedule the meeting for another time?"

Maurice and the pilot exchanged glances. Both seemed a little uncomfortable, as if silently debating what they should say.

"I probably shouldn't tell you this," said Maurice, turning around in his seat. "The truth is, Dr. Mertz wanted to come, especially because he knew there'd be a news crew reporting on it. Unfortunately, the helicopter has a weight limit and we had to turn him down. But what do you say we just stick with the 'important meeting' story?" He winked at me.

I nodded. I have to admit that, for a moment, I felt sorry for Old Glory. How embarrassing.

Higher and higher we rose. I gazed into the billowy white clouds which were so close I could almost reach out and touch them. During airplane flights as a little kid, I fantasized about leaping out and bouncing on them as if they were giant bales of cotton. Learning the science behind clouds in school totally ruined that for me. Still, they looked so fluffy and comfortable, the old fantasies returned.

Maurice reached back and nudged me. "Hey, remember why we're up here." He pointed toward the land. "You should be looking down, not up. Keep an eye out for colored water."

For the next hour or so, the three of us circled Glacial Lake and the surrounding mountains. How spectacular everything looked from above! The glistening lake reflected the white clouds. Rivers and streams snaked through the countryside, and the mountains cast shadows over the land. The thrill of the ride and the awesome beauty left me breathless.

And then I saw them. A brook tinted green. A pond tinged with blue. A reservoir glowing with a hint of yellow.

But no colors spilled into Glacial Lake.

"It was a good plan," said Maurice, "though it looks like we may never know where your fish came from."

The pilot gently settled the helicopter in the same spot from which we started. When the spinning blades came to a stop, I hopped out and said goodbye to the crew. When I was far enough from the aircraft, the pilot tipped his cap, and the aircraft rose like a balloon taken by the breeze.

I trotted over to my parents, Dr. Holland, and the Mishras, who had watched all the action from lawn chairs in front of the deck.

"It was awesome," I gushed, and described everything I saw. "But no dye in the lake. What now, Dr. Holland?"

He had a mug of coffee in one hand, and his unlit pipe in the other. "Maybe we'll try again early next spring when the water levels in the mountain lakes and streams are at their highest."

"I'll be in school," I sulked. "You'll find the home of the Walking Fish without me."

Dad chimed in. "If you can hitch a helicopter ride again, we'll all take a day off from class to come. We'll make it a science field trip."

"Yes!" I said, pumping my fist in the air.

"I'm sorry you didn't get any closer to an answer to the fish mystery," Mom said. Your hair's not in your face, though, so I'm guessing you're not too upset."

I shrugged. "It's a little disappointing, but the helicopter ride was amazing even though the pilot wouldn't let me try out the controls. You see things you can never see from the ground." I paused, remembering one of them. "By the way, there's a cat sunbathing on our roof."

CHAPTER 24

In this dream, a thick brew boiled violently in a giant pot on a camp fire. I stepped closer to see what was cooking. I peered over the rim to discover a Walking Fish trying desperately to climb out of the pot. In place of its blowhole was an eye, which stared at me in a wide, silent scream.

I awoke sweating beneath my thin blanket. It was now early morning. I rose to open the window, letting the cool breeze blow into my room, and climbed back under the covers. Now I lay in bed, tracking a bug with a zillion legs as it crawled from one corner of the ceiling to the other. Something else was bugging me, and I couldn't quite put my finger on it.

Dishes clattered in the kitchen, and soon the sweet smell of fresh baked cinnamon rolls wafted into my room. My stomach growled, yet I couldn't drag myself from bed until I figured out what was gnawing at me. It had to do with water. Hot water. Cold water.

I remembered what Carla had said when I visited the research lab. That first night in the tank at GLU, the Walking Fish appeared to have been trying to get to colder water by hovering near the filter. They had to bring the water temperature down because Dr. Holland suspected that the fish preferred the low temperature.

Everyone assumed it had been washed down from a cave into Glacial Lake, and then became trapped in the pond after the lake receded. I now thought back to all the times I waded or snorkeled in the pond. Why had the water always felt colder than the lake? Shouldn't the pond have been warmer, since the shallow water was easier for the sun to heat?

I've got to check the pond again. I wish I had a thermometer.

Come to think of it, I didn't recall returning the one from the cave a few days before. After the trip, I had stuffed my dirty clothes into the hamper.

"Please, Dad, tell me you didn't do the wash," I hollered as I raced past him to the laundry room.

"Why would I do something like that? I'm not the one who threw an iPhone into the lake. And good morning to you, too!"

In a heap on the floor I found my muddy cave clothes, along with the rest of the week's unwashed clothes. I had not yet done the dreaded laundry, and if I let it go one more day, Mom was threatening to extend my punishment through September. This time, however, procrastination had worked in my favor. I sifted through the front pockets of my pants, finding only a granola bar wrapper. In a back pocket was half of a squashed Milky Way bar. Good thing I found that before it went in the washer. There were only so many times my parents would forgive me for putting chocolate through the wash.

Finally I found the thermometer in my grimy jacket. Within minutes I dressed and darted out of the house. "Back in ten minutes," I called.

"Don't expect your cinnamon bun to still be hot when you get back," yelled my father.

The screen door slammed behind me and I dashed through the yard toward the pond. This time I was not interested in turtles, frogs, or even fish. My only concern was the feel of the water.

I kicked off my sandals and worked my way methodically around the pond, which was now only up to my knees at its deepest point. I checked the temperature in various locations, working my way toward the large boulder where my fish originally appeared. My heart raced as I stepped barefoot into the soft mud at the base of the boulder. Yes, there was still a frigid current coming from beneath that large, flat rock, just as I had noticed the first morning. I plunged the thermometer between my feet for a final temperature reading, but a whirl of cold water around my ankles told me all I needed to know.

I recalled how, on the day I captured it, the fish had attempted to burrow beneath the flat rock in the pond. There was no doubt about it. Cold water continued to channel into the pond from that spot from some hidden place. A place to where the fish wanted to return. A cool mountain stream, perhaps? One that originated in a cave? Such a water source would explain why the larger pond had been shrinking at a slower pace than the smaller one.

I stepped from the pond and glanced down at my muddy feet. There was blood between my toes. I must have cut myself on a sharp stone, but could see no wound. I sloshed my foot in the water to rinse off the soil and debris. A pink hue remained on my skin. This was not blood. It was red dye.

CHAPTER 25

"Darshan and I are going to ride our bikes to the bowling alley," I announced the following morning during breakfast on the back porch. "Then we're going to hang out at the library. Is that okay?" My parents were reading the newspaper and didn't notice my legs bouncing nervously under the table. Dad, studying the stock market page, didn't even look up. Either he hadn't heard me, or he was leaving the plan's approval to Mom. I wrapped my ankles around the chair to still my legs.

"Sure," said my mother. "I'll be out at the museum this afternoon with Mrs. Mishra. You'll have to call your dad if you need anything, since, as you know, I no longer have a cell phone." She eyed me over her reading glasses.

Rub it in, Mom. I cleared my throat and stared into my empty juice glass.

Mom pushed her chair from the table and headed inside with her mug for more coffee. "Do you want some money to buy lunch at the bowling alley?"

I followed her into the kitchen. "Nah, I think I'll just make a sandwich to take along. We're going to have a picnic." I opened the fridge and assembled the bread, sliced turkey, and mustard on the counter, all the time avoiding my mother's eyes. She returned to the porch with a fresh, steaming cup of coffee, leaving me alone in the kitchen. I quickly opened a drawer and removed a small flashlight and a roll of duct tape.

A few minutes later Darshan greeted my parents on the porch. I stuffed a few more things in my backpack and joined him.

"We gotta go now." I kissed Mom's cheek and ruffled Dad's hair.

"Be back before dinner." Mom said.

"Where are you going?" Dad asked.

"Uh! Dad, you never listen."

"What?"

"Always the funny one, Dad. We're going to the bowling alley. Ask Mom to fill you in on the details." I grabbed my jacket from the hook by the door and tied it around my waist.

"It's warm out," said Dad. "Why do you need a jacket?"

"What's with all the questions?" I asked defensively. "Sometimes it gets cold in the bowling alley." I turned away quickly so he wouldn't see my face redden. I wasn't used to all this lying.

I swung my backpack over my shoulder and dashed down the steps. "See ya!"

"What'd you tell them?" asked Darshan.

"Bowling. Picnic. Library. We've got till dinner time."

I anchored my backpack to the rear of my bike with a bungee cord and put on my helmet. Together we started down the road.

"This is crazy," said Darshan. "I don't understand why you don't just ask your dad to take us. Or Dr. Holland."

"I told you, Dr. Holland and his wife are away at a garden show all weekend. My dad would insist on calling Old Glory, who for sure would get Gadi to take him to the cave without me. And I know none of the cavers would take me on my own, even if I knew their phone numbers." I pumped the pedals harder and passed Darshan on the road.

"I still think it's a stupid idea," Darshan shouted from behind. "You said the drive was really long, remember?"

"It only seemed long because I was carsick. The turnoff is a dirt road just past that little bridge a few miles up. We do have to move fast, though, if we're going to explore the cave and make it home in time for dinner."

The road was narrow, but there was a bike lane all the way from the town to the university, and a good deal of the way beyond. With the wind at our backs, we made good time, reaching the dirt road just after noon.

"Get into a lower gear," said Darshan. "It's getting steep." When we reached the spot where Gadi had parked the Jeep a week before, we hid our bikes behind a cluster of bushes and swung our packs onto our backs.

Already tired from the long bike ride, we began the hike up to the cave. We picked up a couple of branches on the way to use as hiking sticks. It was hot even in the shaded woods, and about halfway up we stopped for a swig from our water bottles. Without Dr. Mertz to slow us down, we made it up in half the time of the previous trip.

Near the cave entrance, Darshan and I dug into our overstuffed backpacks for our extra layers. We pulled jeans over our shorts and sweatshirts over our t-shirts.

"Leave your bike helmet on," I said. I tore a piece of duct tape and fastened a flashlight to Darshan's helmet. He did the same to mine.

"Ready?" I asked.

"Ready!"

"Let there be light!" I said, and we switched on our makeshift headlamps. I laughed. "You look like a coal miner."

"You look like a goofy girl with a flashlight taped to a bike helmet."

There was an immediate chill the moment we stepped into the mouth of the cave. It was nice after the heat of the day, but I knew from experience it would soon feel very cold.

"Did you bring extra batteries?" I asked.

"You told me to bring layers, water bottles, a flashlight and a cell phone. You didn't mention extra batteries."

I clutched my head in exasperation. "I did *so* tell you to bring extra batteries."

"No, you didn't."

"Never mind, then. We better pray that these batteries last, or we're in big trouble."

Darshan stomped a foot. "This is stupid. We could get lost in the dark and die in there and no one would even know where to find our bodies. You know what? Forget it! I'm not going." He backed out a few steps toward the sunlight.

With hands on hips, I narrowed my eyes. "Fine," I snapped. "I'll go in by myself." Moving deeper into the belly of the cavern, I listened for Darshan's footsteps behind me.

"Okay, I'll come," he blurted, throwing his hands up in defeat.

I smiled to myself. He was too good a friend to let me go in alone.

Our headlights illuminated the tunnel. I kept my eyes focused, searching for the passage I had seen my last time in the cave.

"It was somewhere around here," I said. "I stopped to get a spider out of my pants. That's when I noticed the hole near the floor. I counted my steps on the way out—about 437, but they were uneven steps, and I might have messed up my count. But it was about ten minutes to the exit."

Rachelle Burk & Kopel Burk

"Before you said it was only five."

"Whatever. Just keep a lookout to the right." I said, not feeling nearly as confident as I tried to sound.

"You said you heard water flowing, right?" said Darshan. "We should listen for it."

"Yes, but I could only hear it when I was actually deep in the side corridor, not from the main path."

We made our way cautiously and quietly. Watching. Listening. It was eerie—too quiet. Creepy shadows danced on the wall from our headlights. I was sure I felt spiders crawling up my leg. Nothing looked familiar.

Still we pushed forward, deeper and deeper into the cave.

"There! That's the passage." It felt narrower than last time, but I squeezed my way to the end. I squatted near the floor. There was no hole. It was a dead end. I backed out.

"False alarm."

Darshan's breathing quickened though he said nothing. As we continued down the main path—at least I thought were still on the main path—I realized I had forgotten to count my steps. Was it much further? Had we gone too far?

Another artery branched off to the right. I took a tentative step in, no longer sure of myself. Darshan followed so close I could feel his body heat. We pressed our way into the short, narrow tunnel a few feet until we reached a stone wall. I pointed to a hole near the ground. It was small, like a ship's porthole.

"Down there." I dropped to my knees and listened. "Do you hear that? I definitely hear water. Let's go through." Darshan joined me on all fours.

Suddenly, something shot out through the hole. It made a breeze as it passed over my head. Its leathery wing skimmed across

134

Darshan's cheek. He shrieked in horror. Now sitting on the ground, he curled over with his arms shielding his face and head.

"You lied! You said there were no bats in this cave!" His voice trembled. I thought he was going to cry.

I placed my gloved hand on his shoulder. "I'm sorry. Honestly, I didn't see a single bat last time I was in here. Simon insisted he's never seen one either. But seriously, Darshan, they won't hurt you."

He swatted my hand away. His headlight shined in my face so I couldn't see his eyes, but I felt them locked on me in anger.

"This is a stupid idea, Alex. Here we are like two idiots, alone in a cave, without backup lights, and not a soul knows where we are. There are bats and bugs and who knows what else in here. What if something happens, like we get stuck, or the cave collapses? Or some rabid bat bites me and sucks my blood?"

His back rose and fell as he panted. If he didn't slow it down, he was going to hyperventilate and pass out.

I kept my tone soft and calm, as if I were speaking to a frightened child. "Listen, you and I are on the verge of an important discovery. If we don't go on, Old Glory will eventually find the home of the fish. Do you want the world to know them as the Mertz Fish?"

Darshan didn't budge. He had curled back into a ball like a roly-poly.

Slowly he lowered his arms. "No."

"So what do you say we complete the mission?" I couldn't believe I'd said "mission."

He sighed deeply. "Okay, you dragged me all this way. I guess we should keep going."

I threw my arms around him. "You're so brave!" Then I flipped onto my belly and, using my forearms, squeezed through the hole into the mystery room.

Darshan was able to stick his head through the hole, but his shoulders were too broad to fit through.

"You don't really think *I* can squeeze in there, do you?" he said. "Unlike you, I'm a normal size person."

"Too bad," I said. "Sometimes it's good to be small. My parents once smuggled me onto an airplane in their carry-on bag."

"Are you serious?" asked Darshan.

"Are you *seriously* asking if I'm serious? Think about it while I take a look around in here."

"Fine."

I scrambled over a boulder and advanced a few feet into the cavern. A brief survey told me that this room was a lot smaller than the one with Teles Lake. Different, but every bit as pretty. A couple of steps to my left was a wavy formation covering a wide section of the wall. I saw some like it in a library book. It resembled draperies made of stone, and I tried to recall what it was called. Oh yeah—"draperies." Duh. I reached out to touch them until Gadi's scolding words flooded my memory, and I withdrew my hand.

Splat! Something landed on my shoe. It looked like a splotch of black tar. I looked up, moving my head so that the flashlight taped to my helmet scanned the ceiling.

A colony of bats huddled upside down in a series of holes above me. A few of them twitched when my light hit them. One let go of its perch, circled the room, and resettled in the spot where it started. I was relieved that Darshan wasn't in here to see them.

Then I discovered the source of the splashing sound that had led me here. A waterfall, two stories high, poured down the wall to my right. It emptied into a pond, the edge of which was only a few steps in front of me. I approached the pool cautiously, as the stones beneath my feet were slippery. They were coated with mud or wet clay. Could this be a sign that the pond's water level had recently been higher? I crouched at the edge and scanned the water.

There was a rock rising above the surface like an iceberg. It was topped with a lumpy black substance, like the stuff on my shoe. As I expected, a cluster of bats hung directly above it. I looked again at the little pile on the rock. *Bat poop.*

Pale stones were scattered in the clear, shallow water near the shore. They were oddly uniform in shape but varied in size. I hadn't recalled seeing rocks like this when I was last in the cave.

Suddenly one of the stones shifted. Then another.

I gasped. The pond was alive with activity. Gliding beneath the surface were countless oval bodies, all with long feelers, foot-like fins, and tiny holes behind their heads.

"Darshan!" I squealed. My voice echoed through the room, startling a half-dozen bats into flight. I slapped a hand over my mouth.

"What? What?" Darshan called from the tunnel. "Are you okay?"

The bats circled the cavern. I held my breath, waiting for them to settle.

"Alex, you're making me nervous. Talk to me! Do you see something?"

But I feared that calling out would disturb the bats again. I would have to whisper the news to him. I rose from my spot and hurried toward the entrance where Darshan waited on the other side. I had only managed a few steps when I slid on a slippery rock and collapsed.

CHAPTER 26

"Oh, God! Darshan, I think I broke my ankle." I was breathless from the sharp, stabbing pain that shot down to my toes and up to my knee. I tried to stand but couldn't, and if I couldn't stand, I sure wouldn't be able to climb up through the hole. Darshan would have to come in and help me. But wait—Darshan was too big to fit through the hole! Realizing this, fear overshadowed the throbbing pain.

"You're kidding, Alex! I know you're kidding. It's not funny."

"I wish I were. It hurts!"

"Geez, Alex, what are we going to do? My mom's going to freak. I can't believe this. We're going to be in big trouble, you know!"

I clutched my leg above the ankle and rocked back and forth. "Maybe we won't," I said. It came out more like a question than a statement. "I don't think they'll be angry when they hear that I've found a whole school of Walking Fish."

I waited for Darshan to answer.

"Did you hear me?" I asked.

"I heard you, but I don't believe you."

"They're here, Darshan, honest!"

I was pretty sure he was hyperventilating now.

"Darshan?"

"That's great, Alex. Really great. But I can't get in to see them, and we have to get you out. Are you sure you can't crawl through?"

I tried again to get up, but putting any weight on the foot caused intense pain. "I can't stand up, Darshan." I gingerly untied the lace of my shoe and eased it off my foot. The ankle was already starting to swell.

Darshan let out a long moan. Either that, or a cow was mooing on the other side of that wall.

"This can't be happening. First my dad is injured and handicapped for life. Now my best friend."

"Dar, I'm *not* injured for life. It's just my ankle. In fact, maybe it's only sprained."

He wasn't listening. "How did I ever let you talk me into this? It was a nutty idea, and I'm nutty for going along with it."

There was real fear in his voice. For his sake I composed myself and said calmly, "Why don't you call my parents, okay?"

"Yes, I'll call them. Good idea." A moment later he said, "There's no cell reception inside the cave. I'll have to go out to make the call. Will you be okay?"

"My ankle hurts, but otherwise I'm fine."

"You're going to get cold sitting still in there. Here, take my jacket." He shoved it through the hole. "Now, hang tight. I'll be quick." He hurried from the cave. I wiggled over on my butt to retrieve the jacket. I tried to keep calm by thinking of the speech I would give when the reporters once again congregated at my cabin.

A few minutes passed and Darshan wasn't back. *Where is he?* I wondered. Maybe he was having trouble reaching my parents. I remembered that our mothers had gone out together, but Dad should be home. What if he had gone out without his cell phone? Darshan would have to call his own parents. His mother would definitely freak out, just as he said.

Too distracted to plan my speech, I started to sing, keeping the volume low so as not to wake the bats again. I continued to watch the pond, scanning the water with my headlight. I bet Teles Lake flowed into this pond. Or maybe it was actually a *part* of Teles Lake, with cave walls creating separate rooms around it. I scanned high up the sides for a crevice like Dr. Holland had described—one that might run all the way through the mountain and into the pond where I caught my fish. But so many cracks covered the walls. Any one of them could be a channel to the outside or only inches deep.

I shivered. I tried to put my shoe back on to keep my foot warmer, but the swelling had increased and it hurt too much. So I focused my attention back on the fish in the pond.

There was a sudden movement on the bat-poop-covered stone. Something had climbed up the side. A frog? No, a frog wouldn't be this deep in the cave. My eyes focused on the creature, which climbed higher until it was mounted like a statue on a pedestal. Two long feelers swayed to and fro.

A Walking Fish! It had crawled completely out of the water, remaining on the rock for a few seconds before slipping back beneath the surface.

For a moment, I forgot the ache in my ankle. My heart pounded. The fish seemed able to breathe out of water, at least for a short while. Maybe that's what the blowhole in its head was for. With a rush of adrenaline, I tried to scoot closer to the pond for a better view, but the piercing pain that shot through my ankle made me crumple. Shivering, I curled up and waited anxiously for help.

Not long after, I heard a man's voice. *How could Dad get here so soon?* I wondered. I was about to call out when I recognized the voice of Dr. Mertz.

"The mineral levels in the pond where the Byron girl found the fish most closely match that of this cave," he said. "She mentioned that she had heard water flowing not far from the cave entrance, so I have a hunch we're close."

Not wanting them to discover my cavern, I switched off my flashlight and sat in total darkness. I was sure Mertz could hear my heart pounding from where he stood.

I trembled from both fear and cold, and clenched my teeth to keep them from chattering. *Where is Darshan?*

Another voice said, "Hey, look. There's a backpack."

I recognized the smooth accent. It was Gadi. *That traitor!*

A faint light moved around the tunnel beyond the portal.

"There's another room back here," Gadi said. "It could be the one Alexis was talking about."

"Go check it out," said Mertz.

A stream of light shone through the opening for several seconds, then disappeared. For a moment, all was quiet.

"The hole is too small. I won't be able to crawl through," said Gadi. "I'll get on my belly so I can at least peek inside."

Soon, a flashlight poked through the porthole. The light illuminated my face. I froze like a deer in a headlight.

"*Imaleh! Mi zeh!*" Gadi exclaimed. "Alexis, what the hell are you doing in there? Do you need help?" As shocked as he was, I remained mute.

"Ah-lex-EES! Answer me!"

I finally blurted, "Okay, okay! Gadi, you won't believe this. There's a pond in here, and it's full of Walking Fish!"

Old Glory boomed at Gadi. "Move aside!" Then he let out a string of cuss words.

Gadi disappeared and soon Mertz's boots appeared in his place. Grunting and panting, he lowered his oversized self onto his hands and knees. His headlamp and pudgy face filled the entrance hole.

"You're lying, aren't you?" he snarled. "There's nothing in there." He squinted, scanning the cavern, but couldn't make out a thing with my light shining in his face.

"I'm not lying. They're here, gobs of them."

That familiar vein appeared on Old Glory's forehead, pulsating with each foul word that escaped his plump lips. "Come out now!" he demanded.

"No!" I yelled. "I was here first. This is my cavern, my pond, and my fish!"

"None of this is yours, you little brat," Mertz said through gritted teeth. "You're a kid playing around, and I'm beginning to lose my patience. I'll make you a deal. Leave right now, and I'll tell no one you were here. It'll be our secret. If you don't, I'll see to it you're arrested for trespassing."

"Oh yeah?" I scoffed. "I'm calling Dr. Holland right now. I'll make sure *he's* the first scientist to see the fish." I turned my back and pretended to punch numbers into a nonexistent phone. "Hi, Dr. H, this is Alex. I'm in the cave and found a whole school of the fish. Come quick!"

"Who do you think you're fooling?" Mertz snarled. "We both know there's no signal in here." Amid more growls and curses, he vanished from the hole.

CHAPTER 27

I heard Mertz and Gadi arguing on the other side, but couldn't make out their muffled voices. And there was a third person also. Darshan was back! No, it sounded like a woman.

Anger replaced my fear and even numbed my pain. Why did Gadi bring Old Glory? And where on earth was Darshan?

Gadi called through to me again. "Alex, it's terribly dangerous to be in here by yourself. People die getting lost or stuck in caves."

"Why did you bring Dr. Mertz here?" I hissed.

"Oh for goodness sake, Alex, he's chairman of the department," Gadi said with exasperation. "He's heading the study. Why shouldn't he be here? He asked Carla and me to guide him back in, so we did."

So it was Carla's voice I had heard. Two traitors.

Gadi then spoke in a hushed tone. "Alex, listen. Dr. Mertz has gone out with Carla to call the police. It's for your own safety. Please, tell me the truth, is there anyone in there with you?"

"I told you the truth already. Darshan was with me, but he went out to call my dad."

"He left you all alone just to tell your father about the fish?"

"No, because I twisted my ankle. I can't get out."

"*Oy,*" Gadi groaned. "You've got to be kidding me."

"Didn't you see Darshan out there?" I asked.

"No. But we took a different route up. The path we took last time was too steep for the professor. How hurt are you?"

143

"I can't put any weight on my foot. And it's getting swollen."

"Other than that, are you okay? Are you cold?"

I squirmed. "I have Darshan's jacket, but I'm freezing. My fingers and toes are numb."

"Here, take this." For the second time in an hour, a jacket was shoved through the hole to me.

"Thanks." I stretched to grab it and draped it like a blanket over my other layers.

"I need to find help for you," Gadi said. "Someone who can actually get you out of there. I'm leaving for just a few minutes, to make a phone call, and will come right back, I promise. Okay?"

"Okay, thanks. Um, Gadi?"

"Yes?"

I was not only suffering with cold, pain, and a bladder that was about to burst, but now my stomach was growling as well.

"My backpack is out there somewhere and I'm kind of hungry. Can you dig inside it and find me a snack?"

He shot through a Snickers bar, and it practically landed in my lap. I munched, shining my flashlight at the water. Another Walking Fish had since crept out and settled at the edge of the pond, feeling around with its long mustache.

A bat pooped into the pond from its roost overhead, creating a tiny splash. There was a brief flurry of activity in the water. The fish on the bank backed itself into the pond and swam to the spot where the droppings had landed.

The fish are eating the bat poop! I thought. If so, it was a food source Dr. Holland hadn't thought of when taking care of my fish. I made a mental note to tell him about it, then stuck the remainder of the candy bar into my pocket. I had lost my appetite.

Gadi returned a few minutes later and assured me that help was on the way. In the meantime, Chief Collins, having been phoned a while ago by Dr. Mertz, was the first to arrive. His face appeared in the portal like a photo in a frame. "You know, young lady, I could arrest you for trespassing. But I think I'll let your parents decide what should be done with you and your friend. Your worst offense here is poor judgment, but that isn't against the law. You sure weren't wearing your thinking cap, were you?"

"I'm sorry, Chief Collins," I said remorsefully. "You're right; I wasn't wearing my thinking cap, or for that matter, my smarty pants either. It was dumb. So, are you going to get me out of here now?"

He coughed out a laugh. "You don't think I can fit through there, do you? I'm afraid you're going to have to sit tight a little longer."

In spite of the extra jackets, I felt colder and more anxious with each minute that passed. Eventually I got word that my father was waiting outside the cave. Since he hadn't known the location of either the trailhead or cave, Darshan had returned to the road to flag him down and lead him up the mountain. That explained why Darshan had been gone so long. *The bonehead could have at least come back to tell me first,* I thought. At least he had gotten help.

The news that my father was out there filled me with a mixture of relief and dread—relief, because I always felt safer with Dad around, and dread, because I knew how much trouble I was going to be in once he made sure I was safe.

It felt like forever until an actual rescuer arrived, though it was probably under an hour. There was a commotion on the other side of the passage. I didn't hear Mertz's voice among them, which was odd considering he always had to be in the center of the action. But Gadi was back, as was Carla, and there was one more

145

voice still too far off for me to make out. I caught bits and pieces of the conversation: "...splint...stretcher...carry..."

Stretcher? They couldn't possibly roll one of those ambulance stretchers through the cave, and certainly not through the tight passage. I wished they would stop talking and get me out of there.

"I'm *ready*," I called out with urgency. "Any time now!"

Next thing I knew, the top of a helmeted head pushed through the portal, followed by a narrow set of shoulders. I laughed out loud because it looked like the cave was giving birth. Soon, the rest of the lanky figure slithered in.

My rescuer stood up and spoke. "Phase one of the rescue mission should take no more than seven and a half minutes."

"Simon!" Of course. Who else could fit through that hole? He folded his arms across his chest, striking a confrontational Superman pose. Who would have thought of Simon as Clark Kent? But here he was, my rescuer, my hero.

"I take it that all my safety instructions last time fell on deaf ears?" he scolded.

"I deserve a lecture, but I hope it can wait till you get me out of here. What took you so long?"

"I'm not old enough to drive, remember? My parents are at work and I needed a ride, okay?"

I lowered my head, ashamed to sound so ungrateful. "Sorry. Thanks for coming."

"Anyway, the Glacial Lake First Aid Squad swung by to get me. They're waiting down below with the ambulance." He looked at his watch, which glowed eerily green in the dark. "Ugh," he grumbled in disgust. "With all this chatter, the mission has fallen 45 seconds behind schedule."

He turned his back to me to reach for something at the opening. Someone began passing supplies through, starting with a narrow, tube-shaped bag, about six feet long, which Simon pulled in and laid on the ground. This was followed by a bright orange first-aid kit. Simon dropped it next to me with a thud. Kneeling near my feet, he opened it and arranged the supplies in a neat row.

"What are you going to do?" I asked. "Will it hurt?"

Simon raised his eyebrows. "It won't hurt *me* a bit." He glanced up and flashed an awkward grin.

Whoa, Simon made a joke. That made me relax a little, but I was still nervous. "Do you know what you're doing? How do you know what to do?"

"Boy Scouts. I also took a course in cave rescue."

"Oh, good. So you've done this lots of times?" I felt a bit more confident.

"No, first time." With that, he took a set of shears from the orange bag and, in two seconds flat, sliced the leg of my jeans from the hem up to my knee.

"What the heck, Simon! You've ruined them!"

It was as if I hadn't spoken at all, much less yelled at him. "Is this where it hurts?" He touched my throbbing ankle.

"Ow! Yes, that's it. Is it broken?"

"How should I know? I don't have X-ray eyes." He placed short, padded boards on either side of my throbbing ankle, securing them with a length of wide, white tape. "This will keep your foot from wiggling around, and that should make it hurt a bit less." He selected a plastic pouch from the equipment bag and punched it once in the center. "Instant ice pack," he said. "Hitting it activates chemicals that make it cold." He jostled the bag for a few seconds to mix the stuff inside. "Hold it on your ankle. It'll help keep the swelling down."

"But I'm already so cold," I complained. Simon shot me an irritated glance, so I set the pack on my ankle between the splints. *I will not whine, I will not whine.*

Simon removed a stiff, rolled-up contraption from the long bag and unfolded it. Several handles were stitched along its sides and ends, and belt straps hooked across the top, middle, and bottom. It resembled a toboggan sled with seat belts.

"You're not putting me in that, are you?" I asked.

"Sure am. It's called a Sked, a kind of flexible stretcher for confined spaces. It was designed by..." I tuned him out, clenched my teeth and held my tongue. *I will not whine. I will not whine.*

Simon lined the inside of the Sked with a thin blanket. "Okay, hop on." He cradled my splinted foot as I scooted onto the thin stretcher.

"Now lie down."

I obeyed. He folded the sides of the blanket over me before clipping the belts across my chest, waist, and knees. When he tightened it, the sides of the device curved up snugly around my body, like I was being rolled up into a tube.

"Don't close it!" I yelped.

"*Now* you're claustrophobic?" he asked. "Don't worry, it stays open at your head."

"Can I take my helmet off?"

"No, too dangerous. There's a risk that you could suffer traumatic injury to your skull during the rescue mission. That could result in a concussion or worse, and the consequences of that—"

"Never mind," I cut in. "I'll keep the helmet on."

Simon double-checked the straps to make sure they were secure. He glanced at his watch. "So far, so good. A minute and a half ahead of schedule, in fact." Grasping the handles on either side of my head, he dragged the Sked, with me inside, to the room's entrance. He heaved it as close to the portal as he could. "Ready?" he called out. "Coming through!"

"Ready!" Gadi replied. His arms reached in, grasped the handles at the top, and pulled. Simon straddled the stretcher at my feet, clutching the handles on either side to prevent it from tilting sideways or sliding down the rocks.

My head slipped through the opening, but the Sked got wedged in at the middle. Gadi yanked and heaved, but it wouldn't budge further. "Pull it back in," he said to Simon.

At any moment, my bladder was going to explode. Each second that passed I regretted more and more having not gone to the bathroom before entering the cave. Another of Simon's lessons that I failed.

I will not pee in my pants. I will not pee in my pants.

Simon eased the stretcher back in. "I have to tighten the belts to make it narrower," he told me.

"I already feel like I'm in a cocoon. How much tighter can you make it?" I began to worry I'd be spending the night in the cave, and imagined them using dynamite to widen the hole. I saw a movie like that once. In the movie, the cave collapsed. *Oh, great.*

Simon tugged on the straps until my thighs squished together and my elbows jammed into my sides. The force squeezed my abdomen like a lemon, and with great horror, I felt a spot of wetness form in my underpants.

"This should do it," Simon called. "Let's try it again."

The device now embraced me so snugly around my chest and belly that I could take only shallow breaths. But it did the trick. As Simon pushed and Gadi pulled, I slipped easily through the gap. Gadi backed out of the short passage dragging the stretcher until it reached the main corridor where Carla waited.

Chief Collins had ordered everyone but those involved in the rescue to wait outside, so only Gadi, Carla, and Simon remained inside the cave to carry me out. It was just as well, since the route to the entrance was not wide enough for two adults to stand shoulder to shoulder. Gadi held on to the straps at my head, and Carla grasped those at my feet. They made their way slowly and cautiously through the cave. Simon followed behind with the first aid supply bag and my backpack.

Carla's eyes met mine. "Having fun yet?" she asked.

I shook my head. "Sorry to put you all through this. I hope you're not mad."

"We're not the ones you need to worry about," Carla said.

When at last we exited the cave, I had to squint against the bright sunshine. Darshan stood nearby, but averted his eyes when I looked his way.

My rescuers settled the Sked onto the ground at my father's feet. He knelt down and kissed my forehead. "You're grounded," he said. "No pun intended."

CHAPTER 28

"What on earth was going on in your minds?" scolded my father. Obviously a rhetorical question, as he didn't wait for me to answer. "Are you both nuts? This was all your idea, wasn't it?" Another rhetorical question. He was on a roll. "I know Darshan wouldn't have done anything this absurd on his own."

I knew it was only the presence of Gadi and Chief Collins that kept him in control. I squeaked out a meek apology. Darshan stood nearby, nervously biting a thumbnail, still refusing to look my way.

"Dad, don't blame him," I said. "It's my fault, like you said. We planned to go in just a little way, and come right back out. I was sure the fish would be there."

Dr. Mertz suddenly loomed over me like a dark cloud. "Oh, and she was right indeed! Only minutes earlier, I had found the cavern with the fish. Little did I know, the children had followed us into the cave." His eyes narrowed to slits above his pudgy pink cheeks and I could read in them the warning: *Don't you dare say another word.*

The chill of the cave had left my body, and was quickly replaced with the heat of anger. That is *not* what happened. Why wasn't Gadi speaking up? I craned my head around and saw him off in the distance packing up supplies with Simon. They were too far away to hear me. Did Gadi even know that Mertz was taking credit for finding the fish? He'd probably back up Old Glory's big fat lie, anyway.

"Darshan?" I called out to my friend. He would tell them what happened! But he only shook his head and walked over to join Gadi. I held back tears.

"Miss Byron," Mertz said, we're all just glad to see you made it out okay. How's that foot?"

I refused to meet his gaze. "Fine."

Mertz slapped a hand on Dad's shoulder. "Kids, eh? No sense at all. Good thing I was there to call for help."

"Darshan had already called for help, thank you very much," I said through gritted teeth.

Mertz chuckled. "That may be, but I made sure Collins dispatched the ambulance. Seems that's what you really need, isn't it? Anyway, I'm sure you're in enough trouble already, young lady, so I'll spare you a lecture from me."

"Yes, I think I can handle the parenting, Professor," said Dad, stone-faced.

Mertz laughed. "Of course you can. Don't be too hard on her, though. She's a great little explorer. But as you see, caves aren't safe places for children to play."

Lucky for him, I was too wrapped up like a mummy to take a swing at him.

Simon announced that we were ready to head down the mountain. "Any chance you can loosen this thing a little?" I asked. "It's hard to breathe."

"Sure thing." He unhooked the straps. "Let's take off those extra jackets, too. Just as fast as you can get *hypo*thermia in there," he gestured toward the cave, "you can get *hyper*thermia out here." Thankfully, he didn't elaborate on the deadly symptoms of overheating. Instead, he helped me pull off two layers. He also removed my helmet and clipped it to the handle of the first aid kit.

I drew in a deep breath. "Ahhh! Thank you, thank you!"

Simon buckled me back in, though more loosely. They carted me down the mountain in the Sked, opting for the longer but less steep path. Gadi and Carla held the handles along one side of the stretcher, while Dad and Chief Collins took the opposite. Simon and Darshan carried all the gear, backpacks and jackets. Not surprisingly, Dr. Mertz walked ahead empty handed. He was soon out of sight.

"How 'bout a little singing to pass the time?" I suggested. *"The bear went over the mountain, the bear went over the mountain, the bear went over the mountain, to see what he could see..."*

The six of them, sweating and panting, did not join in.

"...but all that he could see, but all that he could see..." My voice trailed off and I fell silent, feeling incredibly stupid and childish. I closed my eyes and listened to the crunching of leaves beneath a dozen feet.

At the bottom of the mountain, two paramedics sprinted toward us to relieve my rescuers. They carried me the rest of the way to the waiting ambulance, unhooked me from the hot, confining Sked, and helped me onto the stretcher. A blessedly cool breeze blew over me.

"Where's Dr. Mertz?" asked Carla. No one had seen him since starting the trek down the mountain.

"We drove here in his car," said Gadi. He looked up and down the road. "His car is gone. He wouldn't take off without me and Carla. Would he?" He tried calling Dr. Mertz's cell, but as usual it went straight to voicemail.

"Here, take my car," said my dad. He tossed Gadi the keys and climbed in the ambulance with me and the paramedics.

CHAPTER 29

Late that afternoon, I went home with a plaster cast from knee to toes, a pair of crutches, and a prescription for painkillers. Neither the excitement of the discovery nor concern for my injury softened my parents' reaction to the lies I'd told, or to my "dangerous and downright idiotic behavior." They talked about packing up and heading home, and would not allow me to have any say.

I knew that Darshan was likely in his kitchen suffering through a similar sermon about reckless, irresponsible behavior. I could easily imagine the scene because I'd seen one like it before. Two or three summers ago, while his parents were out, Darshan and I had taken his family's snowmobile for a spin across the field that adjoined our houses. We whizzed through grass, weeds and rocks until the snowmobile clanked and grinded to a complete—and permanent—stop. When his parents got home, we found ourselves seated at the Mishras' kitchen table. Darshan's father just sighed repeatedly and wobbled his head in disappointment. Mrs. Mishra, however, furiously slapped flattened dough in a hot frying pan while delivering a feverish, high-pitched lecture. Then she slammed down steaming mugs of masala tea and a plate of hot chapatti bread and butter. "You two drink your tea, then Alexis goes home. You will not see each other for a week."

Mr. and Mrs. Mishra never told my parents about it.

That evening, my family and I watched the local news in stunned silence. There was Dr. Mertz talking to Leah Burgas, the reporter who had covered the story the day of the helicopter ride. He was puffed up with self-importance, as he recounted his version of discovering the fish.

"On a hunch, based on my analysis of the recent research, my assistants and I entered the cave. I heard water and followed the sound through the passage. When I shined my light through a hole into another room of the cavern, there were the fish, just as I suspected. Though I couldn't get through the hole, I could see the fish quite clearly. One was perched on a rock at the edge of a pond. I was elated. I had discovered the home of the Walking Fish!"

He went on to say that he and his team explored other passages deeper into the cave, and finding no additional tunnels or water sources, made their way back toward the exit. That's when they saw my backpack, and discovered I had forced my way into the cavern with the fish.

"She and the boy had obviously followed us to the cave," said Dr. Mertz. "Very reckless, of course, but kids will be kids."

"That's not the way it happened at all!" I shouted at the TV. I was furious.

"Drop it," my father said. "It's your word against Dr. Mertz's, and quite frankly, after what you did, you have little credibility."

My mother chimed in. "Yes, you've caused enough chaos from this ordeal, so please, just let it go."

I didn't want to let it go. My parents believed Mertz's story over mine. One little lie and they no longer trusted me. Okay, one big lie.

For the next several hours I teetered around the house on crutches, hair in my face, moping and fuming. My parents said they were fed up with my moodiness and went to bed early.

I received my sentence in the morning: we would be cutting our vacation short. They argued that I would be in a cast for the rest of the summer anyway, unable to hike or swim. I begged and pleaded. I even promised to drink lots of milk to heal my bone faster. They said that was nonsense, and besides, I was being punished for what I did, not for getting hurt. The injury was just another "natural consequence."

My mother added, "And let's not forget that Darshan is also grounded for the next two weeks and his parents are pretty upset with you both. So start packing, Alexis. We're leaving Glacial Lake tomorrow."

I dialed Darshan to tell him the news. He didn't answer his cell. I tried his house phone but he didn't answer that either. Although Mr. and Mrs. Mishra would be at work, I was pretty sure Darshan was at home. He was, after all, grounded like me.

I checked online, and discovered he had posted a new drawing: a girl in a cave, belly-crawling through a narrow passage. *That's me!* I thought. *Wow, he's incredible!*

I studied the details of the face beneath the helmet. What expression was he trying to capture? The wide, smiling eyes showed excitement, but there was something else. A touch of... smugness?

I tapped my keyboard and sent Darshan a message. *Dar, awesome pic!*

I waited a few minutes, and when he didn't reply I started packing. My laundry basket was stuffed with clean clothes that I hadn't bothered to put away after finally washing them two days ago. I took my time folding the shirts and shorts, and placed them neatly into my suitcase. I crammed underwear and swimsuits sloppily into a corner of the luggage. The clothes I had worn during my fateful "cave fiasco" were lying stiff with dried mud on the laundry room floor. I stuffed them into a garbage bag along with my mucky hiking boots.

Once more I checked the laptop. Still no word from Darshan. I began to worry that I'd have to leave Glacial Lake without a chance to tell him goodbye.

I typed: *Hey Dar, we have to leave Glacial Lake. Call me.*

He didn't call. Instead, he posted another drawing. This one was of a dark-skinned boy—himself?—glaring from the screen. His face was serious. No, more than serious. Angry.

I typed another message. *Darshan, I'd come to your house but it's hard for me on these crutches. Will you PLEASE come over?*

No reply.

After helping my mother box up the pots, pans, and spices, I said, "Mom, can I go next door for a few minutes? I haven't heard from Darshan since…you know, the cave. I'm getting worried."

My mother frowned and sighed with irritation. "Okay, but hurry back. We still have to clean the cabin before we leave."

"How can I clean? My foot is in a cast."

"Whose fault is that?" she asked, hands planted firmly on her hips. "You'll have to do the best you can."

Grumbling, I hobbled outside on my crutches and made my way slowly across the yard. I used Mr. Mishra's wheelchair ramp to get up to his porch.

"Hey," said Darshan when he came to the door. His voice was flat. Without inviting me in, he pivoted and walked back into the living room, flopping onto the sofa. At least he hadn't slammed the door in my face. I followed him inside.

"I've been trying to reach you," I said.

His jaw was braced and his eyes were hard. It was the same expression as in the self-portrait he had posted. He'd succeeded in capturing the mood perfectly.

"Okay, so now you've reached me," he said coldly.

After a long, uncomfortable silence, I said, "You're mad at me, I know. And I don't blame you. My getting hurt got us both in trouble. Now my parents are making us leave early. That's what I came to tell you—we're heading home first thing in the morning."

I had hoped that hearing this news would soften his anger, but his face remained stony.

I bit my lip, sucked in a breath and rattled on. "Anyway, I'm really sorry for what I did, but this discovery was really important, and—"

"No!" Darshan broke in. He rose from the couch and waggled a finger in front of my face. "If you're going to apologize, there can't be a 'but' in it. Frankly, I'm pretty sure that the only thing you're sorry about is that *you* got in trouble, when what you expected was a big pat on the back." He was trembling. His arms flailed about. "In fact, Alex, I don't think you're sorry about anything at all. Since you only think of yourself, you probably don't even realize what you did."

I moved my mouth to speak, but for the first time ever, nothing came out. I understood how he'd be upset about being punished, but I was confused by the extent of his anger. Shouldn't he be grateful that I let him in on this whole great adventure? Wasn't that worth something? Besides, I was the one with the broken bone, not him.

"What do you mean that I don't realize what I did?" I asked.

Darshan slapped his forehead and shook his head in disbelief. With eyes piercing through me he said, "So I'm right. You really are clueless. Well, let me clue you in, 'friend.' You bullied me into this. I didn't want to go to that cave in the first place. Bats creep me out, so what do you do? You tease me until I give in. You know my mother obsesses about my getting hurt, so what do you do? You talk me into lying to her. I change my mind at the cave and want to back out, so what do you do? You threaten to go ahead without me, knowing I'd never let you go in there alone." He poked my shoulder. "You know what this proves? It proves I care more about you than you do about me. Nothing matters to you besides your big, important discovery."

Then he fell quiet. His arms dropped limp at his sides and his expression relaxed. It was like a storm cloud had suddenly burst, and now, with all the tension released, the soft, puffy clouds returned.

When he continued, his tone was gentle. "You know the only thing that feels worse than being this mad at you, Alex?" He rested a hand on my shoulder but didn't wait for an answer. "What's worse is being mad at *myself* for letting you bully me into all this. Seriously, what kind of friend does that?"

My gaze was fixed on the floor. My heart sank into my stomach and I gripped the crutches so hard that my knuckles turned white. A tear splashed down onto my cast.

"Darshan, I'm sorry. No 'buts.' You're totally right. I was so excited about everything that was going on that I wasn't thinking about anyone else. No excuses. I've been a terrible friend." I swiped the back of my hand across a wet cheek. With pleading eyes, I looked straight into his face. "If you forgive me, I swear I'll never act like that again."

He no longer looked angry, but he didn't look happy either. I knew what was coming: *Goodbye, Alex. Good riddance. Maybe I'll see you around sometime, though I'll try to avoid it.*

It felt like forever before he actually spoke. His tone was strong and uncompromising.

"If I say I don't want to do something, you can't make me feel bad about it."

"I won't."

"And I won't cover for you if you decide to do something crazy, so don't even ask."

"Okay, I won't."

"Ever."

"Ever."

He exhaled heavily and sank back onto the couch, keeping his eyes on me. After a long moment, he asked, "Want a cheese sandwich?"

My heart lifted from my gut back up to my chest. I wanted to hug him, but instead only nodded. "Sure."

That plain old American-cheese-on-white-bread tasted better to me than any grilled-mozzarella-pesto-on-a-multigrain-roll that my mother could have whipped up.

When I got home, I found boxes stacked near the front door, ready to be loaded into the car in the morning. Mom was in the kitchen making dinner, and her big pasta pot was boiling on the stove. She was still in a bad mood, and I wondered how long my parents would stay mad at me.

"Smells good," I said. "Let me guess…Habañero pepper-cream ziti? Portabella ravioli?"

"Spaghetti," she said flatly.

Yikes. Nothing says "Mom's furious" like a pot of plain spaghetti. I decided to make myself scarce and retreated to the living room where Dad had turned the TV to the six o'clock local news.

"Have you finished packing?" he asked without making eye contact. I felt nearly invisible.

"Almost. The only things left are the things I need for the night. Oh, and my fishing gear. It's on the back porch. Will you remind me later to put it in the car?"

"No, I won't. Do it now."

I obeyed, and retrieved my pole and tackle box. Sitting at the dinner table with my icy parents was going to be a real pleasure. I was pondering which would be the lesser evil—a lecture or the silent treatment—when an image of my face flashed on the television screen. It was a photo of me taken from the day the governor was here.

Dad and I exchanged a brief glance, then focused again on the TV screen. A moment later we were watching a recording from Gadi's helmet-mounted camera. Not from the day of the first expedition, but from yesterday's disaster.

It began with a fuzzy image of me squinting in the glare of a light. The video was difficult to make out, but the voices in the audio were crystal clear:

(Gadi) *"Alexis, what are you doing in there? Do you need help?...Alex, answer me!"*

(Alex) *"Okay, okay! Gadi, you won't believe this. There's a pond in here, and it's full of Walking Fish!"*

(Dr. Mertz) *"Move aside!...*(bleeped out expletives)... *You're lying, aren't you?...There's nothing in there."*

(Alex) *"I'm not lying. They're here, gobs of them."*

(Dr. Mertz) "(bleeped out expletives)...*Come out now!"*

(Alex) *"No! I was here first. This is my cavern, my pond, and my fish!"*

(Dr. Mertz) *"None of this is yours, you little brat. You're a kid playing around, and I'm beginning to lose my patience. I'll make you a deal. Leave right now, and I'll tell no one you were here. It'll be our secret. If you don't, I'll see to it you're arrested for trespassing."*

The fishing pole I had been holding clattered onto the wood floor. "Mom!" I shrieked. "Come quick!"

"Hurry!" Dad added.

Alarmed, she rushed into the living room just as the news camera cut to a familiar reporter standing in front of Dr. Mertz's house.

"No one answers the door at Dr. Mertz's home, and calls to his home and office have been ignored," Leah Burgas said. "According to a university spokesperson, the professor has left town on a scheduled holiday."

Anyone with half a brain could see that he was purposely avoiding being questioned about his story. My parents stared dumbfounded at the screen. You'd think the news report was about an alien landing.

"I wonder who tipped off the media," I said.

A minute later we found out when Simon gazed purposefully into the camera. "The rescue mission was successful. The victim should not—I repeat, *not*—have entered the cave without proper equipment and trained guides. It could have ended badly—hypothermia, dehydration, head injury, blunt force trauma from falling rocks—"

"Thank you, Simon." The reporter cut him off to address a man who had been standing just off screen. "And thanks to Gadi Yardin of the Glacial Lake Spelunking Club for providing this revealing video. This is Leah Burgas, with KMB News."

"Oh, my," whispered my mother.

"So, you really *did* discover the school of fish," said Dad. "Well I'll be...."

Two sets of wide eyes locked on me. My mother cleared her throat. "Alexis, you were very wrong in what you did, but I'm sorry we didn't believe you."

I nodded, my lip quivering. Mertz's deception had been exposed and Mom and Dad would forgive me. However, the greatest joy was in realizing that Gadi had not betrayed me.

"Are you crying?" asked my mother.

Sniffing, I shook my head and grinned broadly.

In the end, my parents decided we could stay at Glacial Lake, but I would not be allowed to do anything fun, not even watch TV. A couple of days later Dad said, "Having you around here bored and moping all day is punishment for your mother and me. This isn't fair to us. So…"

I held my breath. This couldn't be good. Time to start packing again?

"…to keep you from ruining our vacation, we're going to let you help Dr. Holland in the Environmental Sciences lab. But first, you have to write a report on everything that happened this summer: your initial discovery of the fish in the pond, the research from the boat and helicopter, and of course, your spelunking adventures. If you do a good job, maybe you can even present it for extra credit to your science class."

At least we weren't going home. Instead, I could look forward to replacing ankle pain with writer's cramp. The truth is, I loved science but hated writing. Regardless, I spent the next several days sprawled on my bed writing a wretched report. Every time I presented it to my father he said, "It needs more detail," or "Check your punctuation," or "You failed to mention how many safety rules you broke." After the fifth revision, I was allowed to work for Dr. Holland.

CHAPTER 30

Following the initial news story, people stampeded to the cave hoping for a glimpse of the bizarre, prehistoric creatures. They'd all be disappointed, for within hours of my rescue, the Parks Department constructed a locked gate at the mouth of the cave. The bars were too narrow for even a child to slip through, but wide enough for bats to come and go freely. Only researchers were allowed to enter, and even they were restricted since authorities wanted the endangered fish disturbed as little as possible.

Dr. Holland phoned me during the time I was writing my report. "We've arranged to collect a few of the fish for research," he told me. "We've learned a lot so far from the one that died, but live specimens can teach us so much more—behavior, diet, breeding habits, stuff like that."

Since they knew of no other spelunkers or OER workers slim enough to slip through the hole, I wasn't surprised to learn who they'd be counting on for this task. Yes, a new "mission" for Simon. No doubt he would complete it in thirty-two and one-half minutes flat, *and* without suffering hypothermia, dehydration, head trauma, broken ankles, or a case of acne.

I had hoped to be working on cool research projects. Instead, Dr. Holland had me filing, copying, and running—or rather hobbling—on errands around campus. I kept hoping to bump into Gadi. He'd risked a lot by blowing the whistle on Dr. Mertz on my account. Finally I asked Carla where he was.

"I really want to thank him," I told her. "And I want to gaze dreamily into those amazing eyes of his." Okay, I didn't actually say that second part out loud.

"He's mountain climbing in Nepal, with a side trip to Sri Lanka for a bit of scuba diving. He won't be back till the fall semester starts."

My heart sank, though it was probably good for him to be far from Dr. Mertz until things blew over.

"I have an email address if you want it, though I'm not sure how much internet access he'll have on Mount Everest." Carla grinned in a way that said she could see right into my swooning heart. I looked away, embarrassed. What would I say to him, anyway? *Thanks for saving my reputation and ruining Mertz's. Now please wait for me to grow up so I can marry you.* In the end, I never wrote to him.

On my third day with Dr. Holland, I bumped into Old Glory in the hallway. He carried a cardboard box overflowing with framed degrees, textbooks, and office supplies. We both froze when our eyes met. I wanted to bolt from the hallway, but it seemed like my feet had become glued to the floor.

A few awkward seconds passed, and Mertz bent down to lay the box on the floor. Expressionless, he took a step toward me. I thought he might slap me.

"Alexis," he said. "I'm sorry."

"What?" I said. He had spoken so softly I couldn't be sure I heard him correctly.

He took a step closer. "I'm sorry for what I did. I was wrong."

I remained stiff. "But why did you do it? Why did you tell everyone *you* found the fish?"

His mustache quivered but the blue vein was absent. He heaved a sigh. I could see that this definitely wasn't easy for him.

"Years ago I was involved in a breakthrough environmental research project that should have been the highlight of my career. It could have landed me a place in scientific history. For five years I worked on it night and day, even to the neglect of my family. Little did I know, a Harvard scientist had been conducting the exact same research. His article appeared in a top environmental science journal the very day I submitted my paper."

Dr. Mertz drew a handkerchief from his pants pocket and dabbed at his moist eyes and sweaty forehead. "When mine came out soon after, no one even noticed. The other guy…he won a big environmental prize."

"That's rough," I said, truly sorry for him. I thought of our own competition, that race to be first, and suddenly understood how high the stakes had been for him.

"Anyway, discovering these fish seemed like a chance to hold my head high again. I'm afraid I lost sight of my own principles and did things I shouldn't have. I regret that."

With his words, I felt my anger dissolve as if a barbed wire jacket had been removed from my back. Hadn't I just spoken similar words to Darshan only days before and been granted the gift of forgiveness?

"Thanks," I said. "I forgive you. I'm sorry, too."

He extended his hand and I took it. "What are you going to do now?" I asked.

"I've handed in my resignation. It's in everybody's best interest that I retire. I'll write a few articles, perhaps. Maybe head out to the coast to volunteer in some ocean cleanup efforts." He patted his round belly and chuckled. "That might even help me get rid of this. Without someone to cook for me, I eat far too much fast food."

I would never see Dr. Mertz again.

Although Darshan was still not allowed to see me, he showed up one afternoon in Dr. Holland's lab. I was feeding the five Walking Fish when I felt his tap on my shoulder.

"Hey, they let you out on parole?" I asked, thrilled to see him.

"More like a work-release program," he said, grinning. "What are you feeding them?"

I handed the Tupperware container to him and he peered inside.

"Dehydrated bat poop. Dr. Holland guessed right about their diet of tiny shrimp, but I told him what I saw in the cave. He's since determined that bat poop is, in fact, another food source for them."

"Yum," said Darshan.

"Did you know bat poop is called *guano*? Why on earth would it need its own special name?" I put the gross stuff into a little refrigerator near the tank and washed my hands. "So what are you doing here?"

"I'm bringing Dr. Holland the first of the illustrations I'll be doing for his new textbook on cave species."

"Whoa! Way to go Darshan! Dr. H never said anything about that."

"I know. I wanted to tell you myself. Can you believe it? Barely in eighth grade, and I'm already a pro! My name will be in the book credits, *and* I'm getting paid!"

I gave him a big hug. "I'm really proud of you, you know. What a summer, right?"

"Yeah. How will we top this one next year?"

"We'll think of something," I said. "Tell your parents to start worrying. Details to follow."

During our last week at the lake, Grandpa came for a visit.

"Let's go fishing," he said.

"Grandpa, you know there aren't any fish in Glacial Lake."

"Heck," he said, dismissing me with a fingerless hand, "I heard they found an alligator in a New York sewer, so maybe we'll catch a fish in Glacial Lake."

"Okay, but what about this?" I lifted my plastered foot.

"Hmm. Looks like someone *cast* an evil spell on you."

"Be serious, Grandpa. Besides, I'm still grounded. Not allowed to do anything fun."

"I am serious. You have a *reel* problem. Tell you what; I'll talk to your folks and promise I won't let you have a bit of fun."

Soon we found ourselves floating on the lake with my cast wrapped in a plastic grocery bag and sealed with duct tape to keep it dry. I put rubber worms on our hooks, since there was no point in sentencing live ones to death for no good reason. We cast our lines off opposite sides of the canoe.

"Watch me catch a tuna," he announced. "By the way, Minnow, do you know why tunas sing off-key?"

"Okay, Grandpa, I'll bite. Why do tunas sing off-key?"

"Because, you can tune a guitar, and you can tune a piano, but you can't *tuna* fish."

He slapped his leg and howled at his own goofy joke. Then he pulled a rolled-up issue of *Fishing Today Magazine* from his back pocket. "Almost forgot," he said. "This just came in the mail yesterday. Check out page 42."

With the fishing pole wedged between my knees, I flipped through the magazine to the feature column about rare, strange fish. The bold title read: *New Species Discovered in Cave.* Above the text was a color photograph of a pinkish-gray, eyeless fish, with two long whiskers and a hole behind its head.

"That's cool, but you know it's already been in a lot of papers. I have a whole scrapbook of the original news reports." I held the magazine back out to him.

"Read it," he said.

I shrugged and read aloud. *"An entire school of cave fish, previously believed to be extinct, has been discovered in a U.S. cave. According to Dr. Julian Mertz, former chairman of the Environmental Sciences Department at Glacial Lake University, this new species is believed to be the oldest surviving prehistoric fish ever discovered. In 1970, a single fossil of this species, determined to be over 400 million years old, was unearthed in the area."*

I waved the magazine. "Really, Grandpa, this is old news to me. And why is Old Glory still getting the attention?"

"Just keep reading," he said impatiently.

"Mertz states that the first living specimen died just days after it was caught by a girl near her family's summer home. The newly discovered species is known to exist only in a single, small subterranean reservoir, which Mertz refers to as 'Byron's Pond,' after Alexis Byron, the young woman who discovered the fish."

I slapped the magazine down on my lap. "Grandpa, he gave me credit! He even named the pond after me!" I squealed with glee and wiggled with so much excitement that I began to rock the boat. Heck, the article even referred to me as "the young woman," not, "the kid."

169

I scanned the page and found the spot where I'd left off. *"The bizarre fish has some characteristics similar to catfish, and to certain classes of eyeless cave fish. However, its unusual combination of features sets it apart from any known genus: Besides foot-like appendages, it possesses a rudimentary blowhole and primitive lungs, which allow it to breathe for brief periods out of water."*

I examined the photo, with lines and arrows labeling its unique parts. A knot tightened in my belly as I recalled the day Darshan and I caught my fish. Images of the boat ride, the helicopter flight, and the cave expeditions—both authorized and unauthorized—flashed through my mind. In spite of all the trouble I had caused, I would miss the excitement.

Grandpa interrupted my thoughts. "That reminds me, Minnow—what do you call a fish with no eyes?"

I waved him off, my eyes still fixed on the photo. "You already told me that silly joke, Grandpa. It's a *fsh*."

"Not this one," he said. He tapped one of his remaining fingers on the page. "Look at the photo caption."

First I read it to myself, then whispered it aloud.

*"Previously dubbed the 'Walking Fish,' it has now been scientifically named **Pedes Alexis**—the Walking Alexis Fish."*

ABOUT THE AUTHORS

Rachelle Burk is a children's author, social worker, clown, and storyteller. She writes fiction and nonfiction for children, including books, magazine pieces, and poetry. Rachelle scuba dives, explores caves, and volunteers on a rescue squad. With her background as a children's entertainer, she's a hit at School Visit programs. Visit her on the web at: www.Rachelleburk.com

Kopel Burk is a retired physician who writes, sculpts, and remains active on the bioethics committee at his hospital. He conceived the idea for *The Walking Fish* over 40 years ago, when he told early versions of the story to his young children, nieces and nephews. His co-author is one of those nieces. At 86, this is his first book.

ACKNOWLEDGEMENT

Special thanks to Terry Cook's
7th and 8th grade literature students
(2013-14) at St. Luke's Lutheran School
in Oviedo, Florida, for your
awesome insights.

MORE TO EXPLORE

PRINT PUBLICATIONS

Bonner, Hannah. *When Fish Got Feet, Sharks Got Teeth, and Bugs Began to Swarm: A Cartoon Prehistory of Life Long Before Dinosaurs*. NY: National Geographic Children's Books, 2007.

Eldredge, Niles. *The Fossil Factory: A Kid's Guide to Digging Up Dinosaurs, Exploring Evolution, and Finding Fossils*. NY: Roberts Rinehart, 2002.

Furgang, Kathy. *Everything Volcanoes and Earthquakes: Earthshaking photos, facts, and fun! (National Geographic Kids Everything Series)*. NY: National Geographic Children's Books, 2013.

Kramer, Stephen. *Caves (Nature in Action Series)*. IA: Perfection Learning, 1995.

Rodriguez, Ana Maria. *Vampire Bats, Giant Insects, and Other Mysterious Animals of the Darkest Caves (Extreme Animals in Extreme Environments)*. NJ: Enslow Publishing, 2012.

Walker, Sally M. *Fossil Fish Found Alive: Discovering the Coelacanth*. MN: Carolrhoda Photo Books, 2002.

WEB SITES

National Speleological Society. http://caves.org/

National Park Service. "Geology, Energy & Minerals." (Information on geology, caves, archeology and more) http://www.nature.nps.gov/geology/index.cfm

Geology for Kids. (Facts, games, experiment, projects, videos, lesson plans and resources) http://www.sciencekids.co.nz/geology.html

Geology.com. "Geoscience News and Information." http://geology.com/

Fossil Guy. "Celebrating the richness of paleontology through fossil hunting." http://www.fossilguy.com/

SPECIAL THANKS TO

Greg Durocher: US Geological Survey, Science Information Services, AK

Patricia Donahue: Junior High School Science Teacher, East Brunswick NJ, and previously with the Department of Environmental Protection (where she used non-toxic dye to trace sewer system water flow).

Dianne Joop: National Cave and Karst Research Institute, Education Director, NM

Linda Green: Program Director, University of Rhode Island Watershed Watch, Department of Natural Resources Science, Cooperative Extension Water Quality Programs, RI (Author of instruction manual for collecting samples using deep water sampling device).

**MORE SCIENCE FUN IS ON
THE HORIZON AT**

TUMBLEHOME
l e a r n i n g

*Whether you're interested in
engineering, dinosaurs, space,
biology, or other wonders of the
universe, we have something for
you. Check out our website for
more **Galactic Academy of Science**
books and other fun and inspiring
THL offerings:*

www.tumblehomelearning.com

G.A.S. SERIES

CLINTON AND MAE'S MISSIONS:
The Desperate Case of the Diamond Chip
The Vicious Case of the Viral Vaccine
The Baffling Case of the Battered Brain
The Perilous Case of the Zombie Potion

ANITA AND BENSON'S MISSIONS:
The Furious Case of the Fraudulent Fossil
The Harrowing Case of the Hackensack Hacker
The Confounding Case of the Climate Crisis

ELLA AND SHOMARI'S MISSION:
The Cryptic Case of the Coded Fair

... and more G.A.S. adventures on the way!